Paul W Robinson

CANDY JAR BOOKS · CARDIFF
2023

The right of Paul W Robinson to be identified as the Author of the Work has been asserted by him in accordance with the Copyright, Designs and Patents Act 1988.

Six Kids Save Planet Earth © Paul W Robinson 2023

Editor: Shaun Russell
Editorial: Keren Williams
Cover by Martin Baines

Printed and bound in the UK by
4edge, 22 Eldon Way, Hockley, Essex, SS5 4AD

ISBN: 978-1-915439-73-4

Published by
Candy Jar Books
Mackintosh House
136 Newport Road, Cardiff, CF24 1DJ
www.candyjarbooks.co.uk

All rights reserved.
No part of this publication may be reproduced, stored in a retrieval system, or transmitted at any time or by any means, electronic, mechanical, photocopying, recording or otherwise without the prior permission of the copyright holder. This book is sold subject to the condition that it shall not by way of trade or otherwise be circulated without the publisher's prior consent in any form of binding or cover other than that in which it is published.

– CHAPTER ONE –

MEET THE CHANS

How did we get into this mess? thought Ingrid as she sat on the floor of the locked cell. Ingrid had pieced together events from talking to her brothers and sisters, and was now trying to make sense of it all. It all started at breakfast time the day before with her mum's odd behaviour…

It was a fine May morning. As the six Chan children came down to the kitchen, they could find no sign of their mum. Instead, they were greeted by an unheard-of feast set out on the dining table. There were heaps of pancakes, piles of bacon, mounds of scrambled eggs, and an ocean of baked beans. There was a tower of toast and enough cereal to satisfy a stable of horses! This was odd enough, but what followed was remarkable.

Six-year-old Mitzi and nine-year-old Dilly were the first down as usual, and they stared like thirsty desert travellers gaping at the mirage of an oasis. Mitzi looked at Dilly. 'It'th not thomeone'th birthday, ith it?' Mitzi had given two of her front teeth to the tooth fairy back in April, so she lisped a lot.

The family had grown used to it.

'No, not until Ingrid's twelfth in September,' Dilly replied. Most of the children had autumn birthdays, their mother's birthday was in January and their father's in mid-February.

Just then their mother popped up. She had been hiding, crouched behind the kitchen island.

'Peek-a-boo,' she shouted. Dilly gave a startled gasp and leapt two feet into the air in shock. Both girls stared, unbelieving. Mum was playing jokes? Dad sometimes did, yes, but not Mum!

Mum had a goofy grin… it looked like it was glued on. Her expression didn't change as she spoke. 'Eat up, my dears!' she trilled. 'Must make you big and strong.'

The girls took their seats at the large old dining table in some confusion. Dilly turned to speak to their mother, but she had disappeared again!

Jacky and Oscar, eight-year-old twins, came in. Once more, Mum 'peek-a-booed' up from her hiding place. This was an even greater success! The twins, who had been arguing and jostling each other as usual, shied like startled horses! Then, distracted by the food, they stared at the feast laid out on the big kitchen table, before scrambling to sit down and dive in.

Ruby and Ingrid entered, arm-in-arm, upright and dignified. Mum had not got tired of her joke; she jumped up once again from below the kitchen counter. The two girls, ten and eleven-nearly-twelve years old, were far too cool to jump! They looked at their mother for a moment, from the height of their combined twenty-one years, and then Ingrid said, 'Don't be silly, Mummy, we are not three now, you know!' Then she said 'Wow!' Forgetting to be cool for a moment, as she stared at the breakfast feast.

'Eat up, my darlings, you need to grow big and strong!'

Ingrid found this very odd. They normally helped to get breakfast ready together. And there had been so much food. Something very strange was going on…

Ingrid surveyed her family, huddled in one corner of the large, empty – and securely locked – room. Desmond their dad, a writer of science fiction stories, and Laura their mum, a book illustrator – and five of their six children, including herself. She sighed as she thought of their lovely old farmhouse home, at the end of the long track, deep in the Yorkshire Dales.

Will I ever see it again? she thought, tearing up. She must not show weakness; she must be strong for the other children!

She looked over at her dad, resting his head against the wall with both eyes closed. Dad's mother and father had moved to England from Hong Kong in 1980. Her dad was thoroughly British. He liked fish and chips, Yorkshire puddings and even builder's tea! But, thanks to his parents, he could also cook a mean garlic chilli chicken with noodles, and he taught his family how to use chopsticks!

She turned her attention to her mum, Laura, the result of a marriage between an African woman of Ibo heritage

– tall and stately – and a blond, blue-eyed Englishman of Swedish heritage – also very tall. Ingrid managed another sad smile as she remembered the wedding photographs, with Mum towering over Dad! On wet days, the children would look through the photos and enjoy a giggle, partly at the old-fashioned clothes, but mainly at the difference in height!

She cast her eyes over her brothers and sisters and put her arms around the boys and held them tight. *With our Asian, European, and African backgrounds,* she reflected, *we look like a United Nations children's meeting. We could describe ourselves as coming: 'in a variety of styles and colours'!*

Only Mitzi, who was six, wasn't there, and Ingrid was desperately worried about her. She always thought of Mitzi as the most remarkable member of their troupe, with her almond-shaped hazel-coloured eyes, coffee-coloured skin, and masses of unruly, curly, brown hair. *But it is not the way she looks that makes her so special, there's just something about her that's, well, different,* thought Ingrid.

Another tear tried to escape when she thought of how they all used to get fed up with Mitzi when she trailed along behind them, or interrupted their games or tried to join in!

Oh, Mitzi! Where are you and what are you doing now? She sighed.

Ingrid's thoughts escaped the walls of their prison, flying out to her beloved Yorkshire Dales, which they all loved to explore – when they weren't in their classroom being home-schooled – and to their farmhouse home.

Ingrid remembered the cosy little room they called 'the quiet room'. She recalled how she had found a stack of old comics in there. Some of the comics were sixty years old. There were copies of *Bunty and Judy*, described as 'comics for girls', as well as *Tiger and Hotspur*, described as 'comics for boys', but Ingrid read them all and enjoyed them all. She loved to lead the other children in pretend games. Thanks to the comics, her brothers and sisters frequently found themselves being led by Captain Ingrid Chan of the Fifth Yorkshire Commandos, or by Inspector Chan of Scotland Yard, or by Head Teacher Ingrid of Greystoke House School!

A sound from outside their prison brought her back to the present. *No more Captain Ingrid,* she thought. *No more games.*

How she wished Officer Zark, Dad's sci-fi hero – an alien police officer who caught alien crooks – would come and rescue them… but he wasn't real!

A day or two before, the children were discussing the possibility of aliens coming to Earth. 'There aren't really aliens though, are there?' eight-year-old Jacky asked Ingrid.

Ingrid looked up from the maths problems on her tablet. 'Course not!' she exclaimed. 'If there were, we'd know about it, silly. We have radar and radio telescopes and satellites and the space station, and, and things.'

Mitzi, clever little Mitzi, wasn't so sure. At that moment she was busy painting her vision of Daddy's alien characters – blobby creatures, with up to eight long arms, each shooting laser guns! They were purple and green and orange, and the guns shot red and yellow flames.

Ingrid couldn't help but smile. Mitzi looked up from her drawing; her hands and face were orange, purple and green too. She was covered in almost as much paint as the paper was!

Mitzi didn't usually say much, but she said, 'If they know how to get here, maybe they know how to get round all the radar and everything ath well?'

Ingrid sighed. She loved Mitzi so much!

And everything was changing.

She was about to go away to boarding school and was starting to realise how much she would miss the old place. She loved sitting by herself in the grass at the top of the hill above the house, with the breeze ruffling her long black hair, and looking down at their beautiful home.

The house was made of grey stone, and it was old – hundreds of years old. In fact, it was so old and weather-beaten, that from her high seat it looked as if it had been sewn out of grey cloth. It was built into the side of a steep hill, great for sledging when there was snow in the winter, and in the summer it was wonderful for rolling down. They would all roll down the steep slope together, getting very dizzy, and feeling extremely sick – in short, having a great time!

From her lofty perch, Ingrid could see the little wooded area just across the track leading to the house. *Just like the hundred-acre wood in* Winnie-the-Pooh, she thought. When Ingrid was young, her mother had read *Winnie the Pooh* to her, sitting on the squashy settee in the quiet room. To little Ingrid, the grove of trees appeared magical and enchanting. But no matter how hard the five-year-old Ingrid searched, she never found Christopher Robin's house, or Eeyore's – not even Owl's!

Ingrid had always enjoyed discovering things and been excited about going away to school – amongst other things it meant that she would finally be allowed to have a phone of her own. But she was also nervous and unsure of herself for the first time in her life.

What would the other girls be like? she wondered. Would they be miles ahead of her in their learning and make fun of her? In any case, it would be wonderful to know that whatever happened at school, her lovely home and her amazing parents and brothers and sisters would be there waiting for her in the Dales, unchanged...

Except... things have really changed now! It looks like there won't be any school for me, she thought despairingly. But even in these desperate moments, her thoughts turned again and again to her youngest sister.

Ingrid wiped away another tear, and hugged Jacky tightly.

'Ow! You're squishing me,' Jacky protested. She apologised, and fussed over the twins, making sure they were as comfortable as possible in their dungeon.

Ingrid looked back at Dad, sitting with his arm around Ruby. He seemed completely dejected. Her lower lip trembled. She controlled it, savagely, and concentrated on her reminiscences.

Now she was a bit more grown up, Dad would ask her for her ideas on his stories. Ingrid was really good at getting the characters out of dangerous situations.

'The engines are wrecked, the crew are injured, and weapons are down. They are surrounded by enemies, what do they do?' he asked her one day.

'Surrender,' she replied promptly. 'Then when they beam their soldiers onto the ship, beam bombs out at the same time. That will wreck their ships, and *they* will have to surrender!'

'That's a bit drastic,' he said and laughed. 'But you know what? I think you've got something there!'

I wish I could think of something to get us out of this, she thought. *I've tried and I've tried, but I can't see any way.*

– CHAPTER TWO –
LOCKDOWN

Mitzi loved being read to. One wet day, when they all went for an 'inside explore', Ingrid found an old copy of *Grimms' Fairy Tales* in the attic.

In the quiet room, she read *Little Red Riding Hood* and *Cinderella* to Mitzi, and she was now in the middle of *Hansel and Gretel*. They had just got to the part where the children were captured, and the witch was trying to fatten them up to make them tastier to eat! Ingrid pretended to stop reading but Mitzi pleaded for Ingrid to read on!

Then came the worldwide COVID pandemic of 2020. No one was allowed to go out or to mix with other people. Schools, pubs, and cafés closed, shops were shut (except food shops), everyone had to wear masks, and households were not allowed to mix for fear of spreading the virus.

Even when Postman Pat (that was what the Chan children called him, his real name was Johnson Mills) delivered their letters and packages, they were left in the porch. Johnson no longer came in for a chat and a cup of tea at the end of his round. Neighbours stopped visiting. It was as if the whole of Britain had put up a notice saying, 'closed until further notice'. No one wanted to catch the virus, it sounded horrible.

None of this affected the children very much. They had each other, they had their house, and they had the Dales.

Ingrid invented a new game. She suggested to the others that during this time, while they had to socially distance themselves from anyone who called at the house, they should pretend they were on the run from the Nazis. They had to hide and stay secret and unseen, just like at the end of *The Sound of Music.*

This game went on for weeks. They had great fun with it. If anyone came to the house they scattered like startled rabbits and hid inside the house, if they happened to be there, or in the countryside if they were out. Mitzi loved this because, although she was too small for many games, at hide-and-seek she was the champion! She was small and slim, and very bendy. She could get into tiny spaces that no one else even considered. None of her brothers and sisters ever found her. Not once!

'Mitzi,' Ingrid said in her head teacher's voice, after she had searched for Mitzi for two hours in vain. 'You must be careful! I read about a game of hide-and-seek one day in a big house, a long time ago. A girl hid inside a box. No one could find her.' She switched to a spooky voice. 'Years later someone opened the box, and guess what they found? The skeleton… of a girl!'

'No!' shrieked Mitzi, in distress. She put her hands over her ears. 'That's horrid! I don't believe you!' But when she asked her mother, she had told her that it might indeed be a true story. 'As I remember it, it was the young woman's wedding day; they were all having a game of hide-and-seek,' she said. 'The bride hid in an old box in the attic, if I remember it correctly, and the lid got stuck. The poor girl was still in her wedding dress when they found her months later.'

After that, Mitzi was a bit more careful about where she hid, but they still never found her!

– CHAPTER THREE –

THE LIGHTS

It was late at night. Everyone was asleep except for Mitzi. She often had dreams, both bad and good, but this one was awful! It was about being shut up in a box. She woke up suddenly, fighting to get out of her duvet!

She lay there in the dark, panting, her heart beating like the whirring wings of the partridges on the hillside when they shot up and away, disturbed by the children's play. Her duvet had slipped to the floor, and she reached down to pick it up.

Ingrid and Ruby, the two oldest girls, had their own rooms. The twin boys shared a room and so did Dilly and Mitzi, leaving one bedroom for guests.

Mitzi looked over to where Dilly lay fast asleep in her bed. Mitzi heaved her duvet back onto the bed, then lay panting for a moment.

Just as she was feeling better and was on the way to falling back to sleep, she saw the lights. She often saw car lights, as her bedroom window faced the A65 road, which was about half a mile away. She was familiar with the pattern. The bright, white, twin headlights would pierce the soft nursery curtains, which were patterned with characters from *Bluey*.

Bingo, Bandit, Chilli, Muffin, Jack, Rusty, Lucky and, of course, Bluey would appear on the far wall above Dilly's bed, then they would track across the wall, disappearing when they came to the corner of the room. Sometimes they went left to right, other times they went right to left, depending on whether the car was going towards Leeds or Kendal.

But these lights were different! For a start there were three instead of two, and they were not white. They were blue, yellow, and green. But the main difference was that Bluey, instead of going left to right – or the other way round – started on the floor next to Dilly's bed and rose slowly upwards! Bluey bathed Dilly and her bed in pale yellowy-greeny-blue light, then floated up the wall, where she came to a stop, right on a drawing Dilly had made of some complicated machine she had invented. Mitzi watched the pretty sight, entranced, her mouth open. The light show lasted for a whole minute (Mitzi counted).

Mitzi was so proud when she was able to count all the way to one hundred. Mitzi counted a lot of things. She counted rabbits on the hillside and stars in the sky. She knew that car lights took between three and four counts to cross the room, and she counted the time while these pretty new lights travelled along their bedroom floor and up the wall. They took a full sixty counts to complete their journey, before disappearing.

Mitzi snuggled back down and lay there for a few minutes, enchanted. The lights took her mind off her nightmare. Her heart rate returned to normal, and she fell back to sleep. She had no more dreams that night.

– CHAPTER FOUR –

THE DAY THAT EVERYTHING CHANGED

Ingrid played through the events of the last twenty-four hours in her head as everyone else tried to get some sleep – as best they could in that uncomfortable place. She was looking for some way out, something she might have missed, the smallest route of escape, any plan, no matter how desperate.

It had been the following morning, after Mitzi saw the lights, that their mother started to act very oddly…

'But, Mummy, you always say how we need to watch our portion sizes!' Ingrid said as their mum urged them to eat their enormous breakfast up.

'That was before! Now I'm saying tuck in! Come on, I've cooked all this for you, be good children and eat it all up!'

Dad was nowhere to be seen. The children assumed he was working in his room; maybe he had come up with a good story idea, so they had indeed 'tucked in' to the biggest breakfast of their lives! The two boys thought this was great, and they stuffed themselves almost to bursting!

While she ate her cereal, bacon, eggs, sausages, toast, beans, tomatoes, and pancakes, Mitzi turned to Dilly and said, 'This is very funny… I mean not funny ha-ha, but what Ingrid would call curiouserer and curiouserer!'

After breakfast, the curiousness continued. Instead of gathering everyone in the room downstairs that the family used as a schoolroom, their mother told them to go out and play.

The twins were only too happy. 'Yay!' they cheered together.

'But, Mum, it's a school day,' commented Ingrid. The boys looked daggers at her. *If looks could kill, I would have been a smoking heap of ashes on the floor,* she thought.

'It's all right for you lot,' she protested, 'I go to school in September. I don't want to be behind!'

'September? Oh, that's miles away! School? Pooh! Go out and play, my darlings. Climb things, run around. Get strong! Lunch is at twelve,' their mother sang out, the grin still plastered to her face.

The boys cheered again. They did not wait – in case their mother changed her mind! They were off like a brace of rocketing pheasants.

Mum shooed the girls out, practically pushing them out of the house.

Once they were all outside, Ingrid called a family conference on the hillside.

'What's this all about, do you think?' she asked the others.

'Dunno and don't care. It's great!' exclaimed Jacky who grinned broadly, before turning to his brother. 'C'mon, Oscar!' The two boys were off, running across the open countryside, along the ridge at the top of the hill, pretending to be aeroplanes shooting at each other, with loud ratatatatata noises, using up the energy the big breakfast had given them.

Ruby rolled her eyes at this childishness. When Ingrid went away to school, Ruby would be the oldest – she would be the big sister. Ingrid suspected that Ruby couldn't wait! She had been practising her big sister skills. They included: rolling of the eyes sarcastically, clicking the tongue in a sarcastic manner, sarcastic remarks, and looking down your nose – sarcastically! She rehearsed them all the time.

The four girls remained sitting in a circle on the grass, warmed by the late May sunshine. They continued the meeting.

'Mum was behaving very strangely this morning,' Ingrid said.

'Oh, yeah, for sure!' Ruby agreed. 'I mean, how immature was that? I mean, totes immature, right? I mean, "peek-a-boo"? Really!'

'Not just the joking around, but no school either? She always says how important it is. And that huge breakfast, already cooked. She usually waits to see what we want for breakfast. A lot of it would be thrown away. What a waste! I didn't know we had that much food in the house.'

'Maybe Mum and Dad have had some good news, and this is her way of celebrating with us,' Dilly said. 'Oh... you don't think she's going to have another baby?'

'But then she would have told us. She told us straight away when Mitzi was on the way,' Ingrid pointed out. 'Do you remember, Ruby? You were only three and you got all excited because you thought it was going to happen that same day. You didn't realise it would be ages before Mitzi finally arrived. Mummy told you she would be the last, and you wanted to know how she knew.'

'You don't think that she's been on the apple wine we all made?' suggested Ruby.

'No!' Ingrid was indignant. 'Mummy never drinks, except sometimes with meals, you know that.' But she had been given something to think about. *It* was *a little bit like Mummy was drunk, especially with that grin!* she thought.

'I thaw thome funny lighth latht night,' Mitzi lisped.

'What lights?' asked Dilly.

'Latht night, I had thith bad dream, right? About being thyut up in a boxth. When I woke up, I thaw thethe lightth, like the carth, you know? But the lightth were, like, all different colourth. There were three of them. They didn't go acroth; they went up the wall. For thixthty countth.'

Ruby reached into the big sister compartment in her brain and pulled out a sarcastic remark. 'I suppose there were purple, orange, and green blobby monsters, too, like in your drawings!'

Mitzi frowned and thought. 'No, no monthterth, jutht lighth. They were yellow, blue, and green. Dilly wath athleep. You were thnoring, Dilly!'

'Mitzi,' said Ingrid, a bit more gently, 'maybe you were still dreaming.'

Mitzi was getting upset now. 'I wath *not* dreaming,' she cried. 'I woke up becauth I wath thcared by my nightmare. My duvet fell on the floor then, when I went to pick it up, I thaw the lighth.'

Ruby reached into the compartment again and dug out a loud and highly effective 'tut'. 'What's that got to do with Mummy?' she said.

'Nothing, I jutht wanted to tell you about the lighth.'

But Ingrid wanted to know more, at least it was something to take their minds off Mummy's strange behaviour. Mitzi's story sounded too detailed to be a dream.

'Mitzi. It's OK. Look, we believe you.'

Ruby tried an eye roll, but her heart wasn't in it. Ingrid was doing 'nice big sister' and Ruby hadn't practised that one!

The boys were rolling down the hill at high speed. They chose that moment to crash into the circle of girls, scattering them. Ruby tutted again. The boys lay there, dizzy, panting and laughing.

Ingrid decided to act. She stood up and clapped her hands to get their attention. 'OK, everybody, listen up. Mum's behaving oddly. We need to keep our eyes open, until we see what's happening. Maybe she's not well.

We'll have another meeting later, and you can all tell me what you've seen and what you think. We'll meet in my room after dinner. And we can talk about how to investigate Mitzi's lights.'

The boys shrugged dismissively. So far, they liked the way their mother was behaving – no school and a huge breakfast! Ruby shrugged sarcastically, and Dilly nodded.

Mitzi whispered to Ingrid to remind her where they had got to in *Hansel and Gretel*; the witch was fattening up the children – to eat!

– CHAPTER FIVE –

OYSTERS AND SEASHELLS

The fateful day continued. Ingrid suggested passing the time by playing hide-and-seek. They didn't stray far from the house. They liked to play the game in and around the grove of trees where there were lots of hiding places. This time Ruby was 'it'.

As usual Mitzi was the last one to be found; she only came out of hiding because she thought it must be getting near to lunch time. Seeing the others all scattered about the trees in a hopeless search, she first smiled and then called out, 'I win!'

The others heard and trooped over to her.

'I don't know how you do it,' said Dilly. 'I'm sure I looked everywhere. I looked behind all the trees, and I even climbed a tree to see better!'

'She's so tiny, she could hide in a matchbox,' said Ruby, grumpily.

To everyone's surprise, Mitzi began to sing, in her high, lisping voice, 'Where the bee thuckth, there thuck I. In a cowthlipth bell I lie. There I couch when owlth do cry…'

The others stared at her, astonished, except Ingrid.

'I taught her that!' she exclaimed. 'It's Shakespeare put to music. I found it on YouTube. We've been singing it. I was planning to organise us all to do a concert.' She gave Mitzi a stern look. 'It was supposed to be a secret!'

Mitzi grinned back at her, showing the gap in her teeth. 'I like it,' she said. 'It'th what I do. I hide inthide the flowerth, then none of you can find me!'

'Don't be silly!' retorted Ruby. 'No one can hide in flowers, not even someone as small as you.'

'Well,' replied Mitzi. 'You can't find me, can you?'

The boys thought the idea of hiding inside flowers was a very funny joke, and they roared with laughter.

'I don't know what you two are laughing at,' Ingrid said, 'you're so noisy that we always find you in ten seconds flat!'

That shut them up!

They straggled back to the house. Mitzi found a grass stalk to chew on. It helped her to think. But thinking only made her worry, so she spat out the grass stalk, and watched the clouds drifting across the blue sky above.

Arriving back inside, they went into the utility room to wash their hands and then went into the large kitchen-diner. When they saw what was on the table their eyes almost bulged out of their heads. There were piles and piles of sandwiches, and heaps upon heaps of cake. There were tuna sandwiches, prawn sandwiches and salmon sandwiches. There were Oscar's favourite cheese and onion rolls, there were ham and pickle, and egg mayonnaise rolls, there were even bacon butties –

using the bacon left over from that amazing breakfast! And then there were the cakes! There was Victoria sponge, date and walnut cake, Bakewell tart, and colourful iced fairy cakes.

'Wow!' breathed Jacky and Oscar almost together.

'When did you get all these cakes, Mum?' Ingrid asked, suspiciously.

'Oh, I just flew down to the shop and got it all while you were outside, then I flew back again!' said Mum gaily.

Scientifically-minded Dilly spotted something new sitting on the corner of the kitchen worktop. 'What's that thing over there?' she asked. 'That machine thing? It's glowing!'

'Oh, it's a new kind of oven, dear. I'm trying it as an experiment.'

'Where's Dad?' asked Ruby.

'Oh, he's terribly busy. I must ask you not to disturb him right now, dear.'

Mitzi looked worried.

She whispered to Ingrid while Mum was distracted as she laid more cakes out, 'She looks like Mummy; her voice is like Mummy's, but she doesn't sound like Mummy. Not really. Mummy doesn't talk like that!'

Ingrid put her finger to her lips.

Nobody else was saying anything, they were too busy eating! In fact, for once, there was silence all around the table, except for Oscar's noisy chewing.

Oscar was suffering with his adenoids, which made his breathing very loud, especially when he was eating.

He was due to have them out, along with his tonsils, but the lockdown had stopped all non-urgent hospital operations.

Adenoids was a new word for Mitzi.

Ingrid liked to try out jokes and tongue twisters on Mitzi. Her sister loved trying the one about the seashells, but it was impossible for her right now, because of her missing front teeth. She asked Ingrid to say it.

'As fast as you can!' she commanded.

'OK, here goes... She sells seashells by the seashore, the seashells she sells are seashells, I'm sure. So, if she sells seashells by the seashore, then I'm sure she sells seashore shells. Phew!' Ingrid got through it without a mistake, but the effort made her pant. 'Now you try.'

'I can't! Lithen. Thye thellth theathyellth... Oh, I can't wait to get my front teeth back!'

'She was a real lady,' said Ingrid.

'Who wath?'

'The seashell lady, she really lived, a long time ago. Mummy told me about her. She was called Mary Anning. She lived by the sea. She dug in the cliffs. Her dog... well, never mind her dog... She discovered lots of important fossils, dinosaurs, and things, but because she was a woman, no one would believe her. So, she had to sell seashells to make a living.'

'Thatth thad!'

'That was the bad old days!'

'Are thingth better now?'

'Better, maybe. Not best!'

'Why?'

'Some men still don't have respect for women.'

'Oh... Why?'

'I asked Mummy that. She said that some men are afraid of women.'

'Why?'

'That's enough "whys" for today,' said Ingrid, who didn't really know the answer. 'C'mon, let's do your favourite poem.' So together they started, 'When I was/wath one I had just/jutht begun...'

Mitzi loved comical poems and rhyming words; she thought that the idea of a noise annoying an oyster was very funny!

Clever Mitzi had made up a poem on the spot:

'What sort of adenoids annoy a boy? Noisy adenoids annoy a boy... and his sisters too!'

– CHAPTER SIX –

THE NEW OLD BARN

After their huge lunch, the children were sent out once again into the May sunshine to 'run around and play'. Ingrid suggested they play French cricket. Nine-year-old Dilly was particularly good at this, and usually won. They had adapted the game slightly, and if you got a good hit on the tennis ball with the cricket bat, you would run between two wickets. These were usually two heaps of coats. Dilly was tall, like their mother, and had long legs. She could run fast, and she made a good score running between the wickets. Mitzi was always getting out, because she couldn't run fast. On the rare occasion she managed to hit the ball, she batted it high into the air and got caught out. But she had fun, too – when the boys weren't bossing her around!

It was a warm day, and after running around for a couple of hours, they were all thirsty. They traipsed into the kitchen to get drinks.

Mum was there.

'Hello, my dears,' she sang. 'Look, I've prepared a picnic for you! Why don't you take it outside in the sun?'

The children looked at each other in astonishment.

There were two hampers on the table. One was full of the cakes and sandwiches that didn't get eaten at lunch, and packets of crisps and biscuits had been added – just to fill up any corners that might be left in their tummies! The other hamper was full of cola and fizzy lemonade. They were not normally allowed sugary, fizzy drinks, so this was clearly a special occasion.

'Mum, is it a special day today? Has something happened?' asked Ingrid.

'Happened, my dear, why should anything have happened? I'm just treating you to a nice picnic tea.'

'But…' Ruby began, and then shouted 'OUCH!' as Ingrid stepped on her foot.

'Sorry, Rubes,' said Ingrid, 'clumsy me! That's lovely, Mummy, thank you. Erm, can't Daddy take a break? It would be nice for him to come outside as well.'

'Daddy's gone out, dear. He won't be back… for some time.'

That means we are on our own then! realised Ingrid.

The children struggled out with the heavy hampers containing the picnic tea and climbed to the top of the hill overlooking the house. As they crossed the yard, Ingrid noted Dad's car was still parked there, at the side of the house.

If Daddy's gone out, he was on foot, and he's not a fan of long walks by himself! Hmm! she thought.

Ruby tackled Ingrid about her sore foot. 'Why did you tread on my toe? It hurt!'

'Sorry, Rubes, but I think the less we say to Mummy just now, the better. She is behaving very oddly. I need to think.'

They all sat and ate quietly. After their games, they were thirsty, so they drank the sugary, fizzy cola and then, worn out and stuffed with food, they lay in the grass and thought.

Something's going on! Ingrid thought. *I think Mummy is ill or something, and where's Daddy? Mummy says he's gone out, but his car is here. Anyway, we're supposed to be in lockdown so he shouldn't be going anywhere. And there's a new machine in the kitchen that I've never seen before, and all those cakes, and she 'just flew down to the shops'. I'm worried, but I don't want to scare the others. And because we're in lockdown I can't go and tell anyone... Oh dear, oh dear, I feel so alone. What can I say? What can I do? I need a plan!* Ingrid tried to calm her whirling thoughts and focus on planning, but she was finding it difficult.

'I wonder why Mummy isn't using our names,' said Mitzi. 'She keeps calling us "darlings" and "dears'."

'Mummy is so childish today! So uncool!' was Ruby's comment. She turned to Dilly. 'I think this top looks good on me, don't you?'

'I think it's great!' said Jacky.

'My top?' said Ruby, pleased.

'No, silly,' replied a scornful Jacky. 'All this food, and no school!'

Oscar was thinking along a similar line to his brother.

'Scrumptious grub! Very fizzy pop!' he said. 'After all that pop, I bet I can belch the national anthem.' So, he did.

Ruby looked at him in disgust! Mitzi and Jacky

giggled, which, of course, only made Oscar worse! Ingrid stood up. There were two mysteries: Mummy's behaviour and Mitzi's lights. She would try and solve at least one of them!

'Right,' she said decisively. 'Listen up. We're all going for a walk. I want to investigate something. But first, Mitzi and I are going inside for a minute. The rest of you wait here. Look at the clouds, what pictures can you see?' She took Mitzi's hand and led her inside while the others lay back on the warm grass and tried to see pictures in the clouds, a game they often played.

'Pretend we're hiding from the Nazis,' Ingrid whispered to Mitzi. 'We're hungry soldiers, and we need to get food from the house, but we mustn't be caught! So, really quiet, and sneaky, ok?'

'OK,' replied her youngest sister. 'Who are we really hiding from?'

'Mummy. I don't want her to know what we're up to just yet.'

Mitzi thought for a moment, then she said, 'Oh. OK.'

They slid in through the back door with exaggerated care. Ingrid peeped through the crack in the door of the kitchen. Mum was in there, busily preparing their next – enormous – meal. Ingrid put her finger to her lips to warn Mitzi to keep quiet, and they tiptoed up to the bedroom Mitzi shared with Dilly.

'Exactly where did you see the lights, Mitz?'

Mitzi climbed onto her bed, and lay down to get the angle right. She got up again and stood in the middle of the carpet, close to Dilly's bed.

'It thtarted here,' she said.

'It thtarted, I mean started, down on the floor?' Ingrid asked.

'Yeth. Then it went all along the floor, over Dillyth bed, and up the wall.'

'Up the wall?'

'Yeth, it thtopped here. I counted. It took thixthty whole countth.' She indicated the drawing on the wall above Dilly's bed, about halfway along, where the lights had come to rest.

Ingrid thought hard. She knelt on Mitzi's bed to look out of the window. She then looked back to the spot on the floor and put out her arm. She pointed to the floor with her right arm then put her left arm up, to make a straight line. Her left arm was pointing out of the window and up to the sky. Then she imagined the lights going across the floor, and her right arm pointed the way the lights went, according to Mitzi. As her right arm came up, finally pointing to the picture on the wall above Dilly's bed, her left arm came down. She balanced on the bed; arms outstretched.

'Look out of the window, Mitzi. Where's my arm pointing to?'

Ingrid pointed her left arm and Mitzi followed the direction with her eyes, looking out of the window and across the green landscape.

'You're pointing towardth Rokeby Farm,' she said.

Rokeby Farm had been in the Rokeby family for generations. It was now run by their neighbours Ms Rokeby and Ms Brackenbury.

'I don't think it could be as far as the farm because the hills would have hidden the lights. So, the lights came from the direction of Rokeby Farm, but not as far as that. Hmmm…'

She put her finger to her lips, took Mitzi's hand again, and the two of them slipped out of the house like ghosts.

When they got back to the others, Ruby was sitting stiffly, her arms folded. On her face was a vinegary expression.

Ingrid sighed. 'All right,' she said. 'What's wrong, Ruby?'

'They,' she huffed, indicating the boys, 'they keep saying they can see rude pictures in the clouds! Its totes disgusting.'

'Booby!' said Jacky, pointing to a small round cloud above.

'Willy!' said Oscar, pointing at another shape.

'See what I mean!'

Jacky pointed to a roundish cloud, with a vapour trail coming from it. 'That one looks like a bottom farting!' He shouted with glee. The boys, delighted with their wit, rolled on the grass, laughing fit to burst.

'That's sooo childish!' Ruby grumbled, and she pulled an eye roll from her sarcasm store.

It was then that Ingrid made up her mind to take the fateful action. 'Come on, everybody,' she said. 'I want to investigate Mitzi's lights. While Mummy is behaving like this, I don't want her to know what we're doing. We're going to see what's going on. We're going on an adventure. We are commandos behind enemy lines, and we're scouting the enemy position, and it's really real... so we have to be 'specially quiet and sneaky. So that means no talking or laughing. And no belching or farting!' she said pointedly, looking at the boys. 'We use whispers and hand signals, OK? Right, we're moving out commando-style. You know what we have to do. Right, Corporal Jacky?'

Jacky knew this game; it was called 'the Fifth Yorkshire Commandos!' He liked it. He nodded. 'We have to keep our heads below the skyline and take advantage of natural cover, Captain,' he said, and he gave a smart salute.

Ingrid wanted to smile, but this was not the time.

'Good, soldier,' she said and saluted back. 'Lieutenant, take the rear, and look after trooper Mitzi!'

'Very good, Captain,' said Ruby, entering into the spirit of the game.

They set off in single file, Ingrid leading, while Ruby brought up the rear, keeping a watchful eye on Mitzi. They ducked their heads down below the top of the ridge and crept down into the valley at the other side. Nothing could be seen there, so they pressed on to the next ridge. Ingrid signalled them to stop just before the summit; then she crouched down and peeped over the brow of the hill. At the bottom of the next valley there was a streamlet, called the Griff. Ingrid scanned the landscape. She knew that the further they walked in this direction, the further away they were into the Dales, and the further from help.

She didn't say this to the others. She signalled for them to move on.

Mitzi came up to Dilly, and they walked side by side. 'Thith ith the furthetht I've ever been from home… exthept in the car of course,' Mitzi said as they splashed through the Griff, not caring about their wet feet on this hot day. Once across the little stream, Ingrid made them all lie down in the long grass while she surveyed the landscape again. There was a large barn halfway up the next rise. It looked like the sort of barn that farmers use for storing cattle feed or hay through the winter. Except it was larger than usual. It was huge.

I don't remember that being there before, she thought.

'Lieutenant,' Ingrid called softly.

Ruby slithered forward through the grass.

'How long has that barn thing been there?' Ingrid asked her.

Ruby frowned. 'It looks enormous. I don't ever remember it being there, Ing, er Captain… though we don't come over this way very often.'

'Wait a minute,' said Ingrid. 'I remember now, I walked this way with Daddy a couple of weeks ago, there was a sort of flat place, like a building had been knocked down, leaving just the stone floor.'

'Looks like someone has built on it now,' shrugged Ruby.

'They must have been very quick then,' replied Ingrid. She gathered everyone around her.

'OK, everyone,' she said in her captain's voice, which was remarkably similar to her head teacher's tone. It also sounded a lot like her police inspector. 'Listen up, Jacky!' for Jacky was lying on his back, searching the sky for birds – or possibly for cloudy boobies. 'This is important, troops. The enemy is inside that barn. We need to see what's in there and report back to headquarters. But we *mustn't* be seen. Is that clear?' Ingrid pressed, but no one replied, and Oscar was looking at a bee on some clover. Ingrid glared and stamped her foot. 'I said, is that clear, Oscar?' she rasped.

'Y-yessir, ma'am,' gasped Oscar. None of the children could remember Ingrid being quite as captain-ish as she was today. This must be serious!

Ingrid surveyed her troops for a minute while everyone looked at her. The boys were no good for sneaking up on the enemy, they would lose concentration and mess about, or they would be noisy. Mitzi was too young; Ruby was looking after Mitzi. That left one.

'Corporal Dilly,' said Captain Ingrid. 'I'm promoting you to sergeant. Come with me, we are going to do a reconnaissance of that building. I think the enemy is in there. So, we need to be really quiet and sneaky, OK? Everybody else, if we don't come back in fifteen minutes, or if we get captured, run away and phone the police! I mean it!' That astonished everyone. Now they knew this wasn't just a game anymore!

'Come on, Dilly!'

Catching the mood Dilly nodded solemnly and, bending double, followed her big sister, and captain, up the slope, towards the danger that awaited them in the sinister barn.

– CHAPTER SEVEN –

THE ENEMY

As they got close to the newly built barn, the two girls dropped onto their tummies and commando crawled through the long grass up to the walls of the building. It didn't look new. The stones were old and covered in moss. As they crept closer, they could hear a strange humming noise, quiet, but persistent. Some of the local farmers had beehives; the noise reminded Dilly of a sleepy swarm of bees on a hot day.

Ingrid signalled Dilly to lie still, then went up to the wall of the building. She put her hand on the wall, it was warm to the touch. *It's not stone,* she thought. *It's some kind of plasticky stuff.* She put her ear against the plastic substance. The whole building vibrated with the humming. It was not loud, but it was shaking the walls.

There were no windows and there was no way to see inside. She went around to the front to see if she could see through a crack in the large wooden doors. She put her eye to the gap where the two doors joined. She could only just see inside the barn. It was as bright as daylight in there, almost dazzling.

It must be full of arc lamps, she thought. *That explains the humming. They must be using an electric generator, like we had to last winter when there was that power cut.*

There were shadows of people moving around. She pressed her face closer to the door to see better when someone loomed up right in front of her on the other side of the door. She was startled and jerked back. She clapped her hand over her mouth to stifle a scream, grabbed Dilly's hand and they ran for it.

To Ingrid's immense relief nobody opened the doors to chase them, no one even shouted. Everything remained as it was before. She sat down heavily in the grass, her heart beating like the wings of one of Dilly's bees. She panted until she got her breath back. It was a while before she could speak.

'OMG,' she said to Dilly. 'They nearly saw me. There are people in there, I could only see shadows, but they looked very strange,' she told her. 'They walked funny. There's a big electricity generator in there, too, and really bright lights. Come on, let's go back.' The two girls slid away and returned to the others.

Ingrid explained the situation to them.

'There's a lot of people in there, and some machinery, but I couldn't see properly. I think something very odd is going on. It's only pretend stone. I think Mitzi is right, this has something to do with the lights she saw. And then there's Mummy! She doesn't seem like Mummy at all, and where's Daddy? And that barn wasn't there a couple of weeks ago, I'm sure. How can they make a new building like that in two weeks?'

'They made it look old, too!' Dilly exclaimed.

'D'you think they're spies?' asked Oscar.

'Or crooks!' exclaimed Jacky eagerly.

'I don't know,' replied their big sister, 'but I think we'd better find out! I'm beginning to think the two things may be connected. We're on our own, we can't go to anyone for help while we're locked down…' She set her jaw, just like Inspector Harding from her comics, when criminals had committed some dastardly crime. 'It's up to us.'

They began the long trek home. By the time they got there the sun had almost disappeared. It was time for the evening meal. They all went to wash and change, and when they came into the kitchen, the table was groaning once more under the weight of the food. Ingrid had read in a book about a 'Lucullan' feast. She looked the word up on the Internet. It meant lots and lots – and lots – of food. Well, this was a Lucullan feast all right! There were tureens full of mashed and roast potatoes, a great steak and kidney pie, dishes full of peas and carrots, a huge jug full of gravy, and a pile of Yorkshire puddings. Once again there was no sign of Dad.

After their busy afternoon, the children waded in with a will, but even Jacky and Oscar were slowing down towards the end. Then Mum brought a great steaming jam roly-poly pudding out of the oven, and plonked it on the table, with another huge jug of custard. They ate what they could, but there was an awful lot left when they began, one by one, to ask if they could leave the table.

After dinner, Ingrid gathered them all together for the meeting in her bedroom.

'We're going back there to that new old barn tonight,' she told them. 'I think you ought to stay here, Mitzi. You can't run like we can. Besides, I need to know there's someone back here to get help if we need it. You know where we are going, if we are not back by breakfast, find someone, Postman Pat, or one of the farmers, and tell them where we went.'

'Thyouldn't I tell Mummy?'

'No! Mitz, I, I don't think Mummy's quite herself at the moment.'

'Who ith thye then?' Mitzi had a way of asking questions that made you think.

Ingrid paused and thought. 'I don't know, Mitz. I think she may be ill or something, but whoever she is, she's not who she was... she's not Mummy anymore. Look, say nothing to her just yet, we'll deal with this on our own.'

Ingrid set her alarm for two o'clock in the morning. She put the alarm clock under her pillow.

She awoke with the first muffled *drrriinng*! She slipped along the corridor from room to room and woke everyone up. Everyone, except for Mitzi, had been sleeping in their outdoor clothes, and they were all ready for an adventure. Ingrid had already packed their backpacks with torches, water and some of the left-over sandwiches and rolls from the fridge.

'I peeped into Mummy and Daddy's room...'

'Were they doing rudies?' Oscar chipped in, and

Jacky sniggered.

'Don't be so immature! There was nobody there, that's the point,' said his big sister, crossly. 'They're not there. Don't you see? They would never go and leave us here on our own. Perhaps the people in the barn have them. If so, we have to rescue them. But you have to do everything I say, or we'll be caught too!'

They all said goodbye to Mitzi and left.

Mitzi was excited by the adventure, but scared and worried at the same time. It took her a long time to get back to sleep, but she did eventually nod off. It felt like she had been asleep for no more than a second when Dilly crashed back into their room.

By now it was four o'clock in the morning. Mitzi looked up at her sister, startled out of sleep, her heart beating nineteen to the dozen. Dilly's eyes were wide with fear, she was panting and ready to drop from running.

'Hide, Mitzi, hide! Don't come out for anyone – not for anyone!' Was all she could gasp before she ran out again, leaving Mitzi feeling scared and confused.

Mitzi threw off the bedcovers and hid as she was told.

– CHAPTER EIGHT –

MITZI ALONE

After a while, in her hiding place, Mitzi heard her mother's voice calling her. 'Come out, little dear!' Mitzi desperately wanted to run to her, but she remembered Dilly's warning, and she waited.

'I've got sweeties for you!' continued her mother's voice.

Mitzi knew that was not right! Sweeties at five o'clock in the morning? She burrowed further into her hiding place, hardly daring to breathe. Next, she heard Oscar's voice.

'Come out, sister.'

Desperate as she was to see her family, Mitzi smelled a trick and stayed put. The next voice she heard was Ingrid, calling all through the house, trying to persuade her to leave her hidey hole. She ignored them all. There was a general noise through the house as 'they' all continued to search for her. Someone was banging on wardrobes, and cupboards. They even knocked on the wooden panelling of the walls in the quiet room.

Time passed and gradually everything quietened down in the house. Outside, the sun rose above the horizon and began its upward journey into the sky. Mitzi stayed put as long as she could, but she began to feel desperate. She couldn't stay where she was for much longer, for one important reason. She needed the toilet!

In the end she had to come out. If anyone had been in the bedroom, watching – and had been on their hands and knees looking under Mitzi's bed – they would have seen a strange thing. First a small finger appeared through a tiny hole in a floorboard, right underneath the head of the bed. Then a little piece of floorboard lifted up and flipped back, leaving a small rectangular hole. An arm wriggled out of the hole, then a shoulder, next a head. Little by little a six-year-old girl squeezed herself out of the hidey hole under her bed. Mitzi had discovered this little space under the floor one day when playing hide-and-seek with her brothers and sisters. Even if you saw the piece of wood, the hole it came out of, and Mitzi climb out covered in cobwebs and dust, you would still say it was too small for anyone to hide in!

Mitzi replaced the floorboard with care.

She looked around her bedroom and listened. The whole place was deathly quiet and seemed deserted. She dusted herself down and thought about what to do next. She eased her window open and climbed out. Normally she wouldn't dare do this, but this wasn't a normal day. The centuries old, weather-beaten stone walls offered lots of hand and footholds. She clambered down to the ground, which wasn't too far, since her room was at the back of the house where the hill was rising up.

Everything was quiet as Mitzi found a place to hide in the garden. After about fifteen minutes she was feeling quite cold. She plucked up the courage and crept back to the house. All the lights were on, but no one was in. *Just like Mummy,* she thought.

Mitzi slid from room to room, peeping through the cracks in the doors by the hinges to make sure each room was empty before she went in. She took off her dressing gown and night dress, then pulled on her play clothes: jeans, t-shirt, jumper and a coat.

She went downstairs and filled a bottle of water from the kitchen sink. She had to stand on a chair to reach the tap, and the tap was quite stiff, but she managed it in the end. Then she took some of the sandwiches from the fridge, left over from the day before, and wrapped them in a plastic bag. She took a torch from a drawer, and the book of *Grimm's Fairy Tales*. She put her haul into her rucksack and quietly left the house, taking one of the walking sticks from the stand by the kitchen door.

She slipped like a ghost into the little grove of trees, and she headed for one of her outdoor hiding places. Using the walking stick she lifted up a curtain of brambles to reveal the opening to an abandoned badger sett, barely big enough for a rabbit to squeeze into. Nonetheless, Mitzi burrowed into it, pulling the brambles back into place behind her with the stick. The brambles were covered in their spring clothes of white blossom. She really was hiding in the flowers! It was dusty and a bit smelly, but it was dry. She settled down in the tiny dark hole, spread out her coat for a ground sheet, and read what she could of the fairy tales, by the light of the torch. She skipped the hard words, but she managed to get the gist of 'Hansel and Gretel'. In the end the children managed to shut the witch in her own oven and cook her!

Mitzi thought about everything she knew. *If Mummy wasn't herself, then she was someone else, like in* Little Red Riding Hood *when the wolf pretended to be grandma.* So, all her family, all the people who came to call her after Dilly's dramatic message, they were all 'wolves' dressed up and pretending. That was how Mitzi saw it, as she lay curled up in her little den.

I hope they haven't all been eaten by the wolves, she thought. She sent that thought away. It was too horrible.

After some time, Mitzi squeezed back towards the entrance and peeped through the curtain of brambles. She saw it was getting late and the sun was past its height. She started to form the basis of an idea. Then, before she knew it, she was floating back to sleep.

But as she fell asleep, she could not help wondering what had happened to the others…

– CHAPTER NINE –

CAPTURE!

After Ingrid's alarm woke her at two in the morning, she sneaked out of the house with Lieutenant Ruby, sergeant Dilly and the twin corporals Jacky and Oscar, leaving trooper Mitzi to go back to sleep.

The small platoon poured quietly over the grass in the dark. They knew the ground well enough to avoid most of the hidden pitfalls, which included holes, rocks and tree roots. They flitted through the tussocky grass. Over the first ridge they went in single file, without problems. In the valley the only light was from the stars above, but they could see a brightness emanating out from the next dale, silhouetting the contours of the hill above. They slid up and over the brow of the hill and they flowed down the dale to the Griff. The water felt so much colder at half past two in the morning. And it didn't dry so quickly, or at all.

They squelched on with wet feet up the hill towards the barn. Ingrid threw herself down onto the floor, signalling for them all to do the same. They rested as she peered through their father's binoculars. The barn was clearly visible. It was all lit up on the inside, and the glowing light leaked out, making it a beacon in the dark night, and ruining their night vision.

'I'm cold and I'm tired,' moaned Oscar to Jacky. 'And my feet are wet. I want to go home!'

'I'm scared,' admitted Jacky.

'I'm scared too,' said Dilly, 'and I feel so sleepy.' She yawned.

Ruby said nothing, but she sat looking at her ruined shoes with a grumpy expression.

Captain Ingrid realised she was losing her troop to poor morale. She needed a speech to inspire them, like in Shakespeare... *Ah yes!* She remembered a speech she had been learning with her mother. She addressed her soldiers:

'Remember, guys, we are doing this for Mummy and Daddy. I think maybe they're in that barn, and we're the only ones who can get them out. I know there's, like, only five of us but, erm...' and she launched into the speech, missing large chunks out, changing it where necessary (and when she couldn't remember the words):

'The fewer men, the greater share of honour!
O he which hath no stomach to this fight,
Let him depart.'
'We would not fight in that man's company...
...Or that woman's...' she improvised.
'...They that outlive this day, and come safe home,
Then will they strip their sleeves and show their scars,

And say "These wounds I had, erm, in May one night."
Old men forget; yet all shall be forgot,
But they'll remember, with advantages,
What feats they did that day. Then shall our names,
Familiar in the mouth as household words—
Ingrid the captain, Lieutenant Ruby
Sergeant Dilly and the valiant twins
Corporals both, Jacky and Oscar.'

Ingrid was quite pleased with that bit!

'Be in their flowing cups freshly remembered.
And we in it shall be remembered—
We few, we happy few, we band of brothers;
Um, and of sisters… er… oh, yes…
And gentlemen in England now a-bed
Shall think themselves accursed they were not here,
Erm, on this adventurous day!'

She finished with a flourish and looked down to see them all, lit by the glow from the barn, looking at her in amazement.

'Wow,' said Oscar. 'That was good, Inge!'

'Shakespeare… Sort of. Look,' said Ingrid. 'Mum and Dad are in trouble. We can't get in touch with anyone, I can't find their phones, I think *they* took them with them, wherever they went, and, and, I'm scared for them. I think they are in that barn, and I'm going to get them! Now, who's with me?'

For her troops, that was as good as the Shakespeare

speech!

Ruby stood up. 'We're all with you, Captain,' she said. 'Don't listen to us grumbling. Come on, let's get Mum and Dad home!'

They all cheered, quietly of course.

Ingrid was pleased that her speech had worked and continued speaking. 'I really don't think Mummy is Mummy. I think it's someone else pretending to be her, but how do we know which one is the real one?'

Everyone thought.

'We know she's not Mummy because she doesn't use our names,' remarked Dilly.

'Names, that's it! Do you remember what Mitzi said, what she saw?'

'Lights?' asked Jacky.

'Bluey,' said Dilly, catching on. 'The shadow from the curtains, going up the wall.'

'Well, I went into the bedroom with Mitzi, and she showed me where Bluey ended up, and I was able to work out the direction of where the lights came from, and this is it. Something landed here and that's where these people are from, a helicopter or funny aeroplane or something.'

'A spaceship!' exclaimed the twins together.

'No, not a spaceship! All right, maybe... but, anyway, we need new names. Code names. We'll be characters from Bluey. I'm Bandit, Ruby can be Bingo, Dilly you can be Bluey and you two,' she hesitated. Jacky and Oscar looked at her expectantly. 'Jacky, you be Chilli and Oscar you be Muffin. Have you all got that?'

'Yes, Captain Bandit,' Dilly said and grinned.

When she had rehearsed everyone in their new names, Ingrid took a deep breath. 'Right. Here we go. Good luck everyone!' she exclaimed.

With that, they all solemnly shook hands and moved cautiously on towards the barn.

The children crept closer and closer. Ingrid went up to the doors to see if she could see what was happening in there. She was rather hoping that the people in there would be asleep, but what they could not know was that the enemy had posted sentries around the barn. They were waiting for them, still and silent in the darkness of the night.

As the little troop neared the barn, they were leapt on by the enemy. They were grabbed and horrible hands, like animal paws, were put over their mouths to keep them quiet.

Ingrid managed to get her mouth free. 'Run, Dilly, run!' she cried. 'Tell Mitzi to hide! Mmf mmf...' Her mouth was muffled again by those strange 'paws'.

Dilly wriggled and twisted like a fish and got away.

Dilly ran like a hare, all the way back to their house. She crashed into her bedroom and managed to gasp out the message to Mitzi, before running out of the house and away. She tried to lead the enemy away from her little sister. The detour into the house had cost her time though, and she was captured. She was at the end of her tether, out of breath, and with a terrible stitch in her side. She had no fight left in her when they grabbed her. Now they were all captured, all except for Mitzi, one brave, though rather scared, little Chan trooper.

– CHAPTER TEN –

INSIDE THE BARN

Ingrid and the other children were taken inside the barn. Their captors looked kind of human, with two legs, two arms and a head, but it was as if Mitzi had been at work with modelling clay. The 'people' were all misshapen with bent backs, and with either one leg shorter than the other, or only one arm. This is why they walked with that odd movement that Ingrid noticed on their previous visit.

Worst of all, they didn't have faces as their heads were covered with a grey hood. They were clothed in loose grey overalls, and you couldn't tell if they were men, women, or something else entirely.

One of the creatures approached them. There were a few moments of utter silence, then the creature groaned, and their features writhed and shifted, until suddenly Ingrid was looking at a terrifying sight. Herself! It was like looking in a mirror. The creature had turned into a perfect copy of her.

The fake Ingrid offered a forced smile, similar to the false mother's rictus grin. 'You will come with us,' she said. 'You will make wonderful food for several of your human days, until we can contact our ships to tell them it is safe.'

'You're going to eat us?'

'Well, yes, but just the children. We're not animals! Your parents were just the bait, but you got here sooner than we thought. We will discard your parents in the morning when we have captured your sisters. We will then have no further use for them.'

The four horrified children were led through the 'barn'. Once their eyes became accustomed to the light, they could take in what they were seeing. Occupying most of the floor area was a huge vehicle. The boys were right. It was not a helicopter; it was a huge tube-shaped spaceship. They were led around the cylindrical shape, which disappeared way down into the floor. Near the top of the cylinder, there were three floodlights. Ruby nudged Ingrid and pointed. Ingrid looked up and nodded. The lights were blue, yellow, and green. *Mitzi was telling the truth all along,* she thought.

They were directed over to a room, with a heavy looking metal door. The fake Ingrid opened the door and pushed them all inside. Ruby gave a cry and ran to a figure sitting on a chair at the end of the room, who stood up to greet them. It was their mum and sitting beside her was their dad. The twins ran over to their dad, and he folded them in his arms.

'Oh, thank goodness you're all OK!' exclaimed Mum. 'I was so worried. But, wait...' Mum scanned all of her children's faces frantically, '...where's Dilly and Mitzi?'

'Dilly—' Ingrid stopped because Dad was frantically waving at her. She looked at him. He put his finger to his lips. He beckoned her and she went over to him and bent down.

'I think they're listening,' he whispered into her ear. 'That's how they got Mummy's voice.'

Ingrid pulled up one of the many chairs, sat down and spoke quietly with her parents.

The other children sat around them and listened avidly.

'We soon saw that she wasn't you, Mummy,' murmured Ingrid. 'She was feeding us so much food, and there was no school, only play, and she was being very silly. Then Mitzi told me about seeing lights through the window the night before you disappeared. I guessed something strange was going on. We came out to investigate and they grabbed us. Mitzi stayed at home. I sent Dilly to tell her to hide, but she hasn't come back. I hope she escaped. What happened to you?'

'I woke up to see them in our bedroom. They gassed us with a sort of gun thing. It sent us to sleep, and we woke up here. Look, I'm wearing Daddy's jeans, and a pair of high heeled shoes! This jumper's mine though.' She stood up to show Ingrid the jeans that were much too short in the leg and too big around the waist. She waved her boots with their vicious-looking high heels!

'Dad got his own clothes, lucky thing! When we saw them later, they looked like us! Dad suspected they might be listening to us, so he spoke in whispers all the time. They couldn't get his voice right, so only one of them went back to the house, as me. I've been frantic, worrying about you all, wondering what they were doing to you. Dad tried to fight them, but there are too many of them. They hurt him. He can't stand up.'

Dad shrugged, 'They damaged my knee. It's getting better.'

'They are taking advantage of the lockdown, my "twin" told me,' Mum continued. 'Now that everything is quiet, and we are all isolated, it's the perfect time for them. They are spying on us and if this group is successful, I'm certain the rest of them will come. They said they are living off the land, whatever that means'

'I know,' said Ingrid quietly. 'Why do you think she was feeding us kids up? Remember "Hansel and Gretel"?'

Her mother looked at her in horror.

'No!' she exclaimed.

'Shh!' said Dad.

'What are we going to do?' asked Ingrid.

'What can we do, darling? There are about twenty of them, and only six of us, four of whom are children. I don't want you to be hurt.'

'I don't want to be eaten,' said Ingrid. 'Hey, wait a minute. Remember War of the Worlds? The aliens were killed by a virus. Maybe COVID will get them!'

'No, darling,' said Mum. 'I mentioned COVID and my twin told me that the aliens are immune to all Earth viruses.'

'Really? That's just not fair!' said Ingrid.

They all sat for some time, trying to think of

anything that might help.

'Come on, Dad! What would officer Zark do?' asked Ruby, referencing their dad's character from his Fredania stories.

'I don't know, Ruby. I don't think he would get himself into this mess in the first place,' was his reply.

More time passed.

Then there was a crash, and the door was flung open. The fake Ingrid stood in the doorway holding a dazed Dilly by the arm. The real Ingrid gave a desperate, disappointed shriek, then ran to her.

'Dilly!' she cried. 'They got you. Oh, we were hoping you got away!'

The stunned Dilly raised her head. She saw two Ingrids, one either side. She was shocked and confused. In that moment, she realised that Ingrid was right. These people could pretend to be anyone they wanted. But which Ingrid was which?

One of the Ingrids spoke.

'OK, Bluey?'

Relieved, she pulled away from the false Ingrid and turned to her sister, who gave her a big hug. The fake Ingrid left, and the great door clanged shut. Ingrid signalled Dilly to keep her voice down.

'I told Mitzi to hide,' Dilly panted. 'They didn't get her. They looked all over the house, pretending to be Mum and Dad. They even pretended to be you, but she stayed hidden. They gave up. It's daylight out there now, and they've all come back. They made me walk back with them. I think most of them went off somewhere to sleep. They left some on guard, though.'

The real Ingrid nodded.

Dilly went on. 'Seeing the fake Ingrid next to you, Ingrid, you can really tell the difference. The fake moves in an odd way. She takes a second or two to change her expression. That explains Mummy's funny grin!'

The tired children curled up on the floor and they all tried to sleep. All except Ingrid, whose mind was still whirling, mulling over what had happened, looking for a plan.

Outside, the sun climbed into the sky. *It must be day by now,* she thought. *All we need to do is find Mitzi, avoid being eaten, and stop an interplanetary invasion. That's all!*

– CHAPTER ELEVEN –

TROOPER MITZI SALLIES FORTH!

Mitzi awoke in the old badger sett – curled up like a dormouse in its den, with her coat over her for a blanket. She drank some water and ate two of the sandwiches, then peeped out of her hidey-hole. Through the screen of brambles, she could see that the sun was now gone, and it was twilight out there.

I'm scared, she thought. *Where is Dilly? Looks like I'm all on my own.*

That was a sad thought, so she sent it away for now until she could deal with it.

I'm the only one left – Trooper Mitzi. But what can I do?

Instantly she made up her mind. She packed up her rucksack, which was not easy in that narrow little hole, and wriggled her way out, dragging the bag and her coat behind her. She pushed aside the bramble curtain with her walking stick, then threw her backpack out. As she squeezed through, she got stuck. This frightened her until she remembered a *Winnie the Pooh* story. Pooh sits in his hole eating honey until he gets so fat that he gets stuck trying to get out!

I shouldn't have eaten those sandwiches, she thought.

But the thought made her smile and calmed her down. She was only stuck for a second. She wriggled and writhed, she pulled and pushed, and then she was out. She carefully replaced the brambles because you never know when you need a good hiding place!

Once out, the first thing she did was put on her coat. The next thing she did was head back to the house so that she could use the loo. She climbed up the wall and in through her bedroom window and went to the bathroom.

As she was washing her hands in the bathroom, she heard a noise outside. She crept into Mummy and Daddy's bedroom, knelt down by the window, and, lifting her head up just enough, she peeped carefully out. She could see some sort of car or something out there, and some people beside it. She recognised them. It was the two ladies from Rokeby Farm, Millie Rokeby, and Rosie Brackenbury, with their big old Land Rover.

Thank goodness! She would run downstairs and ask them for help. What a relief it would be to hand the problem over to a grown-up.

She took a second, closer peep. What were they doing? They were carrying things out of the house. Mummy and Daddy's things, and the children's stuff. *Rosie and Millie wouldn't do that!* she thought. *Not Rosie and Millie. They must be more 'wolves'! But why do they want our stuff?*

A desperate idea came to her. She would follow the trail. Follow all the stuff! She had no time to think. Leaving her rucksack behind, she climbed back down from her bedroom once again and crept quietly around towards the front of the house and to the Land Rover. When the two 'women' went back into the house to get more stuff, she ran to the car and crept into the back. She saw lots of clothes and various bits and pieces. They seemed to be taking anything and everything. One of the things she saw was Daddy's bag. It was a bag he used when he had to go to a meeting and stay in a hotel – his overnight bag.

As quick as a wink, Mitzi unzipped the bag and slipped inside.

The fake Millie and Rosie returned and started up the car.

Mitzi had hidden in this bag before; it was another one of her hiding places in the house – if she couldn't get to her bedroom. None of the other children even considered it as a hiding place; they never thought you could hide in a bag! She had worked out how to open and close the zip from inside. She covered herself with a towel that was in the bag. It was dark, she was all squished up, and she could hardly breathe. She hoped that the journey wouldn't take too long.

The Land Rover's doors slammed, then it started to move. It bumped and jumped along the track leading from their house. Things became smoother for a while, and Mitzi realised they must be on the main road. Then it got really bumpy! Mitzi found herself thrown around in her dad's overnight bag. First, she was the right way up, then she was on her side, then upside down, then the right way up again!

It's just like what I imagine being in a – ouch – tumble dryer would feel like! We must be going over the grass – ow! she thought dizzily.

At long, long last the van came to a halt. Mitzi didn't have a plan for what she was going to do next. She was just 'playing wait and see'. That was what their mother said when they asked what was for dinner! 'Let's play a game called "wait and see",' she would say. That was another thought that made Mitzi sad, thinking of Mummy. So, Mitzi sent that one away as well.

The Land Rover stopped at last. Mitzi heard the doors open, and there were noises to show the van was being emptied. She daren't show herself, because the 'wolves' would be coming backwards and forwards to the car moving all the children's and Mummy's and Daddy's stuff. She couldn't let herself be captured. She was the only commando left! So, she stayed as quiet as a mouse. The bag was grabbed towards the end, and she felt herself being lifted up and carried along. There was a last big, and painful, BUMP as the bag was put heavily down, then silence and darkness.

Mitzi waited a while. She counted up to a hundred.

Nothing happened.

Then she counted up to a hundred again. When still nothing happened, she carefully poked her head up, just to take a peep. The bag was lying on its side. It was completely dark out there. She unzipped the bag all the way and climbed out. She was bruised, stiff, and sore, but she stretched and twisted and shook herself. She could move all right. She found she could kneel up.

Above her she could feel a heavy plastic lid. She gave it a tentative push. It moved. She pushed as hard as she could and stood up. There was a crash as the lid fell open. She was standing on a pile of her family's things, all thrown in a heap. This included Jacky and Oscar's dirty socks!

Yucky! she thought. *Why would the wolves want those?*

She saw where she was standing by the light of a bright, full summer moon.

It's a big rubbish bin, she realised. *Like the ones outside the shops in Kendal, but clean.*

In the moonlight, Mitzi could make out more of their stuff. There were Ingrid's things: her tablet, her clothes, all mixed higgledy-piggledy with Oscar's football boots, Dilly's art stuff and Mitzi's toys.

She clambered over the side and stood on the grass. There didn't seem to be anyone around. She turned full circle and jumped as she saw the barn, glowing bright in the night. She ducked down behind the bin. She waited a while, hardly daring to breathe. When no one appeared, she decided to take a chance. Taking her courage in both hands, she crept towards the large building. Just then, there came a loud banging noise. Mitzi raced back to the bin and dived into its shadow, her heart thumping, not daring to move a muscle. *Have they seen me?*

In their prison, Ingrid looked up as one of the clumsy aliens pushed open the door and dragged in a trolley. 'Food. Eat!' it said in a throaty rasp. Ingrid's eyes darted around, weighing up the possibilities. She tenderly shook herself free of the twins and moved casually over to the trolley, which gave her a chance to peep outside. Unfortunately, there was another alien outside holding a vicious looking gun, watching for any wrong move. There was no one behind him.

Dilly said a lot of them had gone to sleep, she thought. *I wonder how many are left?*

'I will come back soon. Eat fast!' growled the 'clay man'.

Ingrid took the plates stacked on the trolley, opened the containers, and served the food to her family. She took Dad his food and gave him a long questioning look.

Mitzi continued to crouch, ready to jump back into the bin if anyone came. No one did. She stood up and peeped around the corner. The banging noise began again. Mitzi flattened herself on the floor. From there she could see underneath. Standing right up against the barn there was a big steel thing, like a huge box. The banging was coming from there. She hesitated. She really didn't want to get any closer to the scary barn. She took a deep breath, picked herself up and crept silently towards the metal container.

She put her ear to the metal wall. Now she could hear voices shouting.

'Help, help, get us out of here!' The voice was too muffled to be recognisable, but Mitzi's heart soared at the thought that this might be Mummy, or one of the others shouting.

At the near end of the box was a huge door. Mitzi stood in front of the door and calculated in her head. She reckoned it was about three Mitzis high, and the same wide, so it was a square. She walked along the side of the box. It was twenty steps long. The double door took up the whole front of the box. It had a big bolt.

She lifted up the heavy bolt and tried to pull it across. It took her three goes, with a rest in between each go, but she finally got the bolt free. She pulled hard, but the door was too heavy for her to open. She just stepped back to have a think, when to her horror, the door slowly started to open from the inside.

– CHAPTER TWELVE –

RUN!

After thinking hard for so long and coming up with nothing, the arrival of the food had awoken Ingrid's brain, and given her the glimmerings of a desperate plan. She approached her father.

Seeing her questioning look, he asked, 'What is it, Ingrid? Do you need the toilet? It's over in the corner through that narrow door.'

'No, Dad. Do you remember when Officer Zark and Sergeant Drape were locked in the cell by the alien gang?'

'No. Oh, wait a minute. You don't mean…'

'Yes!' said Colonel Ingrid of Space Patrol. 'We're going to get out of here.'

She paused for a moment to check the invisible space laser at her hip, before going on to explain her plan.

Mitzi threw herself down behind the rubbish bin. She peeped around the corner. The door continued to open, with a horrible metallic *creeeak*. Then a head peeked out. It was a head and a face that Mitzi recognised, despite the mask it was wearing. The last time she had seen this head, it was on a body that was loading her family's stuff into a van. It was Millie Rokeby.

Millie's head turned this way and that. She cautiously emerged from her cell. Behind her came Rosie Brackenbury, similarly masked. The two women were holding hands to give each other courage.

They don't look like fakes, Mitzi thought, as she watched the women emerge. *They're wearing masks. Do aliens need masks? I'm not sure, but they do look sort of normal. I think they're the real Millie and Rosie… I hope.*

She was desperate to hand the situation over to an adult, and quickly made up her mind. She stepped out and showed herself.

The two women were startled, but then Millie said, 'Why, it's little Mitzi. What are you doing here, luv? All by yourself?'

All Mitzi's sad thoughts that she had pushed away came back. Tears came into her eyes, and she began to cry.

'They got Mummy and Daddy, and Inge, and Dilly and Ruby… an' Othcar and Jacky. They came for me too, and I hid. Then I thaw you two with your van. You were taking things from our houthe.' Mitzi was full on crying now, with great big sobs.

'They stole our Land Rover?' asked Rosie. Mitzi nodded.

'And they look like us?' asked Millie.

Mitzi nodded again. She was beginning to quieten down, and was gasping for air in that sort of hiccupping way that you do when your crying is nearly over.

'They got Mummy and Daddy firtht,' Mitzi

hiccupped. 'Then one of them pretended to be Mummy, and tried to make uth eat, like loads of thtuff.' She hiccupped again. 'An', an' then Inge went with the otherth to thee what wath happening in thith barn thing, but they never came back.'

Millie and Rosie gave her hugs and comforted her. They dried her tears and wiped her nose with tissues that smelt strongly of a powerful perfume.

'We've been stuck with those creatures for two days, but luckily Millie has a secret weapon.' She held up a bottle of perfume and a hankie. 'She found out by accident that those creatures don't like her perfume much! It makes their eyes explode!' she said. 'So they shut us in here and they've left us alone.'

Mitzi smiled at the idea of the alien's eyes exploding.

'Rosie, too much information! She is a child, you know.'

Rosie ignored her, and with a wave of the hankie she said, 'Come on, we'll help you look for your family, but be careful.'

'Really?' Millie said. 'We've only just escaped and... Hey look, there's our Land Rover.'

'They wouldn't be so stupid to leave the keys in it, would they?' Rosie asked.

'Oh, never mind the keys. I can start that old thing without the keys if I have to,' Millie replied. She edged towards the car.

'Hang on, what about Mitzi's family?' Rosie said, standing in the way of Millie.

'I think they mutht be in there,' said Mitzi miserably,

indicating the glowing building next to them.

'Just a minute,' said Millie, who pushed past Rosie. She opened the door and rummaged around behind the seat. She pulled out a pitchfork and a shovel. 'These might help.'

They crept around the building looking for a way in but could find nothing. After walking all the way around they returned to the front door.

'Now what do we do?' asked an exasperated Rosie.

In their prison, the Chans gathered around Ingrid to listen to the plan.

'I don't know, Inge,' whispered Mum. 'It sounds very dangerous to me.'

'More dangerous than being eaten?' said Ingrid.

'Well, I see your point,' said Mum. 'All right, Inge, we'll show these guys they can't mess with the Chans!' With that she took off one of her 'killer' high heeled shoes.

A few minutes later, they heard shuffling footsteps approaching the door. Mum and Dad stood behind it as it swung open. An alien walked in past them. It picked up the tray, loaded with empty dishes. It turned, only to find its way blocked by Ingrid and Dilly.

'When are you going to let us go?' demanded Colonel Ingrid. The alien shimmered and turned into a copy of her. In her voice it replied, 'Never.'

While the alien was focusing on maintaining Ingrid's form, the others started to talk at the same time. The alien turned from one Chan to another, half-changing into Dilly, then into Jacky. Some of the half-changes were funny, like when the alien was halfway between Jacky and Dilly. Then Dad came limping into the fray and grabbed the confused alien from behind. He wrestled it to the ground. The other alien spotted the disturbance and pattered in, in its strange lope. As he went past Mum, who was still standing by the door, she swung the high heeled boot hard at his gun arm. The stiletto heel dug into his arm. He squealed and dropped his gun. Inge threw herself at the alien's back. It looked like the alien was giving her a piggyback. Soon Mum and Ingrid both wrestled the alien to the ground, while it kept trying to change shapes to throw them off.

Finally, they managed to subdue both of the aliens. 'Quick, shoelaces!' shouted Colonel Ingrid.

Ruby quickly removed her shoes and reluctantly took out her laces. They were sparkly. 'It's not fair,' she said. 'Why does it have to be my laces? I really like these. Why can't you use your own laces?'

'I'm quite busy at the moment,' Ingrid said, her elbow rested on the alien's face.

'Ruby, they need to be strong. I'll buy you some more,' shouted Mum.

'OK, but I want the same ones. Sparkly like this.'

'Just do it,' shouted Mum.

'Fine.' She pulled the laces out and tossed them to her mum, who was definitely not an alien – not with *that* temper!

After tying up the aliens, the Chans cautiously peeped out of the door. The disturbance didn't seem to have brought any more aliens out of their lair.

'There's the front door!' said Dad.

They slowly moved towards the door, with Mum helping Dad along on his bad leg. Ingrid was in front, and the door was ahead. Just when they thought they would escape, Ingrid was thrown back by some invisible force.

'Ow!' she cried as she was flung to the floor.

'Oh no,' said Dad. 'It's a force field. We're trapped!'

'Now what do we do?' moaned Ingrid, almost in tears.

They all slumped to the ground, waiting for someone to have an idea.

Outside Mitzi, Millie and Rosie circled the building once again.

'What'th that?' asked Mitzi, pointing.

Rosie followed Mitzi's small pointing finger and squinted. 'It looks like a very faint light,' Rosie said after a minute and then turned towards Millie. 'It's coming from the bottom of the wall over there, can you see it?'

'Oh, yes, I see it too!' exclaimed Millie. 'What can it be?'

'I think it's steam escaping from somewhere below.'

They headed towards the shimmering spot.

'Help me,' said Rosie, and she started to dig at the turf with her spade. Millie joined in, scrabbling at the grass with her bare hands. It was very loose, and soon they had scraped away all the turf. It was covering a grill. They all peered in through the bars. There was strong light below.

'It doesn't look too far to drop. All we need to do is

get this grill up,' said Rosie. Millie grabbed the spade and levered it under the metal bars, and they all pushed down on the handle.

After much hard work they managed to lift the grill and push it right back. Millie was the tallest and she leaned through the opening to have a look around. 'There's nobody about. It looks like a big circular room,' she said. The light was so bright it was hard to see how far down the floor was. She took a deep breath and lowered herself into the hole – then, closing her eyes, she let go and dropped. She had to laugh as she fell a mere six inches to the floor, landing easily on her feet. Millie steadied Rosie as she came down, then they grabbed Mitzi as she dangled from the ceiling above them.

The three of them crept across the circular room.

'Oh my!' exclaimed Rosie.

'Will you look at that!' said Millie. Mitzi just stared open-mouthed. Above them stretched the inner workings of an alien spaceship, its engines above their heads.

'If they start them up now, we're toast,' she remarked. 'What's that humming noise?'

'They're using some sort of electric generator,' whispered Rosie. 'It must be that big machine thing, over there. Come on! There's a staircase.'

'I wonder what's in that cupboard,' said Millie. 'Look. It's not even locked…'

'Come on, Millie, this is no time to explore!'

Cautiously, they made their way up the stairs. Millie held the pitchfork in front of her, just in case. Rosie had the spade over her shoulder, while holding Mitzi's hand with her other hand.

Three pairs of eyes peeped over the top stair. There was no one to be seen. Suddenly the most fearful noise broke out. Three heads swung as one in the direction of the racket.

'There's a fight, Rosie. Come on!' cried Millie.

And she was off, up the stairs and across the floor towards the din. Rosie and Mitzi followed, more slowly. Just then the Chans appeared, running, or hobbling in Dad's case, across the floor from left to right in front of them, towards the barn's main door. They watched in astonishment as Ingrid was thrown back, as if she had been grabbed from behind by an invisible hand.

Mitzi was overjoyed to see them all, and ran over to them; but all she could manage to say in her excitement and relief was, 'Hello."

'Mitzi, oh, Mitzi, darling. You went to get Rosie and Millie, you clever thing!' cried Mum. 'I'm so glad you're safe!'

'Not for much longer if we can't turn off this force field,' said Dad loudly. 'Millie, Rosie, can you find the generator and put it out of action somehow?'

The two women nodded and slipped back down the stairs. For five tense minutes there was silence. Ingrid was hopping from foot to foot in her anxiety. Then WHOOMPH! there came an almighty explosion from somewhere deep below them, and a strangled cry. The lights went out and left them all in total darkness.

'Erm… I think the force field is down,' said Dad. 'Mitzi, where are you? Keep talking and I'll find you.'

'When I wath one...' Mitzi recited her favourite poem, and Dad found her in the dark. He grabbed her into the biggest hug of her life.

A light appeared downstairs – the creatures were coming! Mitzi freed herself from Dad's arms and crawled to the top of the stairs, searching for Rosie and Millie. 'They're coming!' she called. 'They're using a torch. Rosie is helping Millie. It looks like she's hurt.'

The two women appeared, climbing slowly up the stairs. Rosie was supporting Millie, who looked dazed. In the torchlight they could see that her hair was standing up like a dandelion clock, and her eyebrows were smoking.

Rosie looked at them and said, 'We found the torch, and some other useful things in a cupboard down there.'

'No time to explore, eh? Ow, ouch!' groaned Millie leaning on Rosie.

'How did you turn the power off?' asked Ingrid.

'It was Millie. I was so proud. She did the bravest thing I've ever seen.' Millie pretended to be embarrassed, and Rosie hugged her.

'She attacked the engine with the pitchfork,' she said. 'She smashed it right into the workings. I guess you heard the explosion.'

'We did,' said Mum.

'Millie flew across the room.' Rosie's lip trembled. 'I thought she was dead!'

Millie looked up. 'Look what it's done to my best pitchfork!' she said. She held up a bent and sorry-looking fork, still smoking. They couldn't help but laugh at her forlorn expression.

'Come on, let's get out of here. Now, where's that door? Can I borrow the torch?' Dad said, snatching it away without waiting for an answer. He shone the beam of light at the wall and eventually found the door. It looked like something you would find in a bank vault.

'Strange, it looks like a barn door outside,' said Rosie. 'I hope it's the right one.'

Suddenly. Lights came on. This was followed by a loud alarm,

'They have emergency lights,' said Dad.

'Quick,' shouted Dilly.

'They're coming!' said Ingrid.

'Here!' said Rosie. 'These might come in useful.'

'Oh, I recognise those,' said Dad, taking the items. 'These are the gas guns.'

'Not "gas guns" any more, "perfume guns"!' said Rosie. We took out the gas cannisters and filled them with 'Passionate Nights'

'What are you going to do, smell them to death?' sarked Ruby.

'Just try it, you'll see! Come on, Millie,' said Rosie, 'let's get that door open.'

'How?'

'You could try turning the handle.'

'Here,' said Dad, tossing one of the three gas guns to Mum, and one to Ingrid.

Rosie pulled hard at the handle, but it would not move.

A door crashed open on the other side of the barn, and five of the aliens appeared. They lurched towards them.

'They're unarmed!' shouted Ingrid. 'Dad, they haven't got weapons!'

Dad waved the guns at the aliens. 'Keep back!' he said. They hesitated. There was a crash from behind. 'Got it,' cried Rosie. Beside the door was an entry pad. Rosie had smashed it open with the spade.

The two women forced the door wide open.

The aliens regrouped and lurched towards them again.

'Fire!' shouted Dad. The perfume sprayed out towards the aliens, who made awful high pitched screams and shuffled off, hiding their eyes.

'Run!' shouted Dad.

Ingrid stayed beside him. She emptied her spray, and then they ran for it following the others. Ingrid watched her mother run like a sprinter in her high heeled shoes, holding Mitzi's hand in one hand and the waistband of her trousers in the other (so they wouldn't fall down). Dad pushed through the pain in his knee and hobbled along as best he could.

Rosie hotwired the Land Rover, started the engine and they all climbed in. She put her foot flat to the floor and the Land Rover shot off over the grass at high speed. They were free!

Behind them the siren was still sounding.

'Is that for us?' asked Ruby.

Rosie paused the Land Rover at the top of the hill, and they looked back down at the barn. A fire seemed to have broken out, and suddenly there came an explosion, followed soon after by another one.

'Erm, maybe not!' said Ingrid. 'I think they're in trouble.'

'Tut-tut. What a pity. Never mind!' said Rosie. She engaged the clutch and drove off.

It was two o'clock in the morning by the time they reached the Chan house, exactly twenty-four hours since Ingrid set off with her commandos. Everyone was exhausted. The adults held a meeting in the big kitchen. To the children's delight there was hot chocolate for everyone.

'Now, Mitzi. You rescued us. Tell us the story,' Mummy encouraged.

'Well. We knew the wolf wathn't you, Mummy,' said Mitzi.

'Wolf?' everybody questioned at once.

'Yeth. Wolf. Like in *Little Red Riding Hood*. He dretheth up ath grandma, thee?' And everyone agreed there and then that 'wolves' was a good name for the aliens.

Mum laughed and hugged Mitzi.

'I don't think people will believe we were kidnapped by aliens,' said Dad. 'Can you imagine the phone call to the police?' Then he put on a silly voice:

''Ere, Dierdre, man 'ere says 'e was kidnapped by aliens, it's not April Fools' day, is it? Hur hur hur?'

'Tell 'im to get off the line, Ursula!'

'I think we taught them a lesson,' said Ingrid. 'Do you think they'll be back, Dad?'

'I think as long as we're in lockdown, we're in danger.'

Colonel Ingrid turned to her patrol. 'We'll have to keep our eyes open, troop,' she said. 'Look out for any unusual behaviour; watch people's faces for strange expressions!' The children all grinned. They could see lots of new games coming up.

They went upstairs and got ready for bed. Before they went to sleep, Ingrid held a meeting of her own, in her bedroom.

'Everyone, I give you Space Cadet Mitzi. Now promoted to Ensign Mitzi. You were amazing, Mitzi!' They all applauded.

The children turned to their smallest sister, only to see that Mitzi's eyes were closing, and she was sucking her thumb – a sure sign she was about to fall asleep.

To everyone's surprise the twins offered to take her to bed. The boys gave her a 'fireman's chair' to her room, and Dilly tucked her up and kissed her goodnight.

Everyone was exhausted and soon all of the Chans were in their beds fast asleep. Neither Dilly nor Mitzi, nor anyone else was awake to see three lights shine on the wall over Dilly's bed and then cross the floor towards the window before disappearing at high speed.

When the Fifth Yorkshire Commandos, Chan division, investigated the barn days later, all they found was a big hole in the ground and some rubbish bins in the middle of the fields. Rosie and Millie went over in the Land Rover and managed to retrieve and return most of the Chan family's belongings.

'Remember, Space Patrol: eternal vigilance!' was Ingrid's final word on the subject.

– CHAPTER ONE –
THE CHANS GO SHOPPING

For a time in the summer and early autumn of 2020, the lockdown was eased. People in England were allowed to go out again and not just for food and other essentials.

One warm July day, the Chan family piled into their Ford Tourneo eight-seater car and set off for the nearest town: Kendal. The whole family was excited. They had been cooped up in the house together for months. Their mother, Laura, needed to buy some clothes for the children, especially for Ingrid, as she was off to school in September, as well as things for herself and the others. Ruby was looking for some new clothes as well; it was such hard work keeping up with fashion!

Ingrid wanted to get some things for school: PE equipment, writing things, a nice pencil box. The twins, Jacky and Oscar wanted some toys and games to play, and Mitzi wanted a new Baby Cries doll. She already had Baba, and Dee-Dee, now she wanted Buttercup… or maybe Dozy, the unicorn doll or… Oh, it's so difficult to make up your mind when you are six! So many dollies, so little time – and so little money! She only had enough money for a small one, like Baba.

'Right, masks on everybody!' said Desmond, their dad.

'Must we, Dad?' grumbled Jacky.

'Yes, you must!' said Mum. 'Pretend you are superheroes or something.'

They all had home-made masks.

It was Ingrid's idea. She had suggested that they make them out of bits of cloth that were in the 'useful box'. The boys used fabric that looked like army camouflage, as did 'Captain' Ingrid. Ruby used a flowery fabric, so did Dilly. Mitzi's mask was pink. They all put them on, being sure to cover both mouth and nose, and off they went to the shops.

Ingrid went with her mother and Ruby. The others went to the Toyland toy shop with their father.

The toy shop was overwhelming. There were so many things to look at. Like a guided missile, Mitzi homed in on a beautifully arranged display of Baby Cries dolls. The boys ran off to the section on handheld videogame consoles. Dad was interested in the electronic games too. He went with the boys. Dilly was looking for some new items for her 'Young Engineer' set. Or, even better, a new chemistry set. She was trying to choose between a kit for making helicopters and aeroplanes, or a chemistry set, when Mitzi came running over to her. Mitzi jigged up and down, and tugged Dilly's sleeve.

'Dilly, Dilly, Dilly! OMG! I want the Baby Crieth doll I've just theen. You must thee it, come, on, come on!'

Dilly sighed, put down the engineering kit, and allowed herself to be towed to the display.

'You must thee it. Its eyes move and everything!'

'All dolls' eyes move, Mitz,' said Dilly.

'No, they don't not Baby Crieth. They cry, but their eyes stay open, but thith one blinks, and itth eyes move all by themselves!'

They arrived at the display, and Mitzi pointed. 'There… oh, it'th gone…'

'Maybe somebody bought it, Mitz.'

Tears filled Mitzi's eyes. She had fallen in love with the dolly at first sight. In desperation she searched all around the Baby Cries display, without any luck. There was nothing there, except that behind the stand, she found a large-ish dolly lying face down, looking very forlorn, without its clothes. It was a sad sight, and it was not 'her' dolly. Her desperate eyes roamed further.

'There she is, there!' cried Mitzi. Dilly followed her little sister's pointing finger. There was a doll perched on top of one of the cases. It was a big one. It was dressed like the other Baby Cries dolls in a onesie with animal ears. This onesie was purple and yellow and had mouse ears.

'I don't know, Mitz, it looks expensive. I don't think you'll have enough money.'

'Thomeone's moved it,' said Mitzi. While they watched, the doll sat, gazing out into the store with her beautiful green eyes. Then, very slowly, the doll did something that made Dilly gasp.

'You were right, Mitzi, it blinked, did you see?'

'Yeth. I told you!'

'I can't reach. You stay here, I'll get Dad or somebody. But Mitz, you won't be disappointed if it's too much money, will you?' She looked at her younger sister, who had stars in her eyes, and sighed, before going off to find someone tall enough to reach the dolly.

Mitzi gazed at the doll with eyes full of love. She saw it blink twice more before Dilly came back, towing a shop assistant with her. The man, wearing his surgical mask, reached up and using two hands, he lifted the dolly down.

'Wow, it's heavy!' he remarked as he handed it to Dilly. 'Be careful, don't drop it!'

The doll was two feet tall, more than half the size of Mitzi. Dilly gave it to her, and she clutched it to her chest in delight. She was panting with effort by the time they got to the checkout.

The young woman at the checkout, behind glass, smiled at Mitzi.

'That's a pretty dolly, isn't it?' Mitzi nodded, too excited to speak.

'Let's see how much you owe us.' There was a barcode attached to the dolly's onesie. Goodness!' she exclaimed. 'It must be on offer. Such a big dolly and only £15.00!' Mitzi couldn't believe it. She had saved her pocket money all through the weeks and months of Lockdown. When she came into the shop, she could afford only the smallest of the Baby-Cries dolls, and now she had this lovely big dolly… for only fifteen pounds! She put the dolly on the floor and handed over the hot sweaty twenty-pound note she had been clutching in her fist. She received the five-pound note of change like a duchess.

The boys had spent their money on new games for their handheld game consoles, and Dilly paid out for her

C500 'Young Scientist' chemistry set. They went back to the car, to wait for Mum and Ingrid.

Meanwhile, Ingrid and Mum were queuing up to pay for their things in the clothes shop. Items like the school blazer had to be bought online from the school's own outfitters, but things like the grey pleated skirt, grey trousers, white blouses and so on, they could get from anywhere.

'I'll put your name in them before you go,' said Mum. Ingrid smiled nervously, and her mother gave her a cuddle and a kiss on the head. She knew that Ingrid was anxious about her new school. 'Tell me how you're feeling,' she said.

'A bit scared,' admitted Ingrid. 'But I'm excited, too.'

'Yes, I remember that feeling,' said Mum.

'Did you go away to school?'

'Oh yes. Not your school, of course. I lived in London then.'

'Did you miss Granny and Gramps?'

'At first, very much – and there were no video calls in those days, not even mobile phones. We had to queue up for the payphone with the other girls. First years, that's year sevens, got to use the phone on a Monday. Everyone got two minutes. That's not much time! But in my time at that school, I made a lot of friends. Friends who I still talk to. And over time I even began to enjoy being there. So will you. There came a Monday when I didn't phone home, because I was too busy with my friends! Your grandma was very worried! I got a strongly worded letter from her, and I made sure to call her the next week! Here we are. You pay for your pencil case, and I'll pay for the clothes. Now, speaking of mobile phones.' Laura handed Ingrid a box. 'You can open it when we get outside.'

As they were lining up to pay for everything there was a text alert on Mum's phone. It was Dad.

WRU? Back at the car. CU soon.

In Q. Checking out. GTG.

Ingrid and Laura paid for their purchases and went outside.

'Let Daddy wait, darling. Open your present.'

Ingrid opened the box. Inside was a lovely new shiny smartphone. She could hardly believe it.

'Oh, Mum!' she cried. She sniffed. 'Oh, thank you, Mum!' She threw her arms around Mum in a big hug.

'You will need it when you are away at school, but you need a bit of time to get used to it, so Daddy and I decided you should have it now. I've put the number in my phone. You should learn it as soon as possible, though.'

They joined everyone back at the car. Mitzi couldn't wait to show her sister and her mother her new doll.

'Wait until we get home, darling,' said Mum, 'then I can see it properly.' She put on her driving glasses, put the car (the children called it the 'bus') into gear and they set off for home.

– CHAPTER TWO –

LILY

Back home, Mitzi showed everyone her new dolly. She insisted that everyone admire it and say how pretty she was. Then she struggled with it up to the bedroom.

The others were just as excited to try out their new things. Ingrid spent some time setting her new phone up in her bedroom, then she put in some of the contacts from her mother's phone, including Millie and Rosie from the farm.

'That doll looked expensive,' said Mum when Mitzi had disappeared with her new pride and joy.

Dilly was sitting next to Mum at the dining table in the kitchen, busy opening her chemistry set and examining the contents. 'They only charged her fifteen pounds,' she said.

'Is that all? I think it must be some sort of mistake. Should we contact the shop?'

'They did look at it carefully. The assistant said it must be a special offer,' Dad remarked.

He and the boys went off to the lounge to play their new Super Mario games. Mum shrugged, got out her drawing materials, and put on her reading glasses, ready for work.

Up in her bedroom, Mitzi was arranging a tea party. She set out all her dollies, including the two Baby Cries dolls. She didn't use the names the manufacturer had given them. She called them Jemima and Sally. She called her new Dolly, Lily after Gran.

She sat them all down around a cardboard box she was using for the tea table.

'Now, today, I am going to teach you about manners,' she said. 'So, Jemima, Sally, and Lily, when you drink your tea, you mustn't thlurp. It's very unpleasant for other people. Now say, "Yes, Mama'."

She picked up each of the dolls in turn and held it to her mouth and said 'Yes, Mama' in different tones until she came to Lily. Lily was a bit too heavy to lift, so Mitzi bent down to speak in her ear. She took a breath, but before she could say 'Yes, Mama' in her best dolly voice,

Lily spoke:

'Yes, Mama,' she said in a sweet dolly tone. Mitzi was first startled, then delighted. 'OMG!' she panted in her excitement.

She ran out of the bedroom and flew down the stairs. She found Dilly in the kitchen. Dilly was reading the instructions for some chemistry experiments in her new set. Mitzi startled her by grabbing her arm, and then dragging her up to their bedroom.

'She spoke,' panted Mitzi. 'She spoke, she spoke. She

said, "Yes, Mama". I think she copieth what you thay!'

She towed Dilly behind her like a small tug pulling a ship. When they got to the bedroom, Mitzi let go, and Dilly entered the room under her own steam. The dolls were just as Mitzi had left them.

Breathless from running Mitzi panted, 'Say, "yes Mama"' into the dolly's ear. There was no response. She tried again several times in different tones, getting louder and more frustrated all the time. Nothing.

'She *did* thpeak!' wailed a disappointed Mitzi.

'OK, Mitz, if you say so,' said Dilly. 'Now can I get back to my chemistry set, please?'

And she went.

Mitzi was left in the bedroom alone with her dolls. 'Why didn't you speak?' she asked Lily with a pout. And she poked her.

'Yes, Mama,' said Lily.

Maybe she only speaks when it's just me, mused Mitzi. So, she asked Lily:

'Do you only talk to me?'

'Yes, Mama.' There was a delay before she spoke. It seemed Lily needed time to listen and work out her answer.

But this was even better in a shivery sort of way. It was a little secret she could keep between her and Lily. *The people who made Lily must be very clever,* she thought. *How does she know I'm on my own?*

By now it was teatime for real, and Mitzi heard her mother calling her down.

'Put your toys away, Mitzi, and come and wash your

hands. It's time for tea.' Mitzi had a big toy chest. She hastily threw all her dolls in there, except Lily, who was too big and heavy to throw around, so Mitzi dragged her over to the toy chest. Using all her strength she lifted Lily up onto the lid of the chest.

'You sit there, Lily, and I'll come back after tea,' she said with a puff.

'Yes, Mama,' said Lily.

After tea, Mitzi scrambled back upstairs as fast as she could go. With hard work and a lot of puffing and panting, she managed to get Lily onto her bed. Pushing Lily's chest and legs, she managed to straighten the dolly so that she was lying down.

'There now, Lily, you're all nice and comfortable, aren't you?'

'Yes, Mama!'

Your onesie is very pretty, isn't it? You have mouse ears.'

'Yes, Mama!'

I'll come back after CBeebies is finished!

'Yes, Mama.'

– CHAPTER THREE–

MITZI'S DREAM

That night, Mitzi watched *Bedtime Stories* and had her hot chocolate. She got into bed and snuggled down with Lily.

'Night night, Lily.'

'Night night, Mama.'

Mitzi was too sleepy to notice that Lily had changed her words. Very soon she fell asleep. She dreamed, as she often did. Mitzi's dreams were usually nice, but she sometimes had nightmares, and this was one of those.

She was running away from some people she couldn't really see, but she knew they were behind her. To her astonishment, next to her was Lily. They were running for their lives, but Mitzi didn't know why, or who from.

'Hide, Mama!' said Lily. They ran to the toyshop, where they both pretended to be dolls until the bad people, whoever they were, had gone. That was when Mitzi woke up covered with sweat, and with the bedclothes all churned up from her dream running.

Mitzi turned her head to find Dilly looking at her from across the room.

'You OK, Mitz?' Dilly asked sleepily.

'I had a nightmare,' replied Mitzi. 'Me and Lily were running away from somebody… where is Lily?' When Mitzi had gone to sleep, Lily was on the bed next to her. Now she was nowhere to be seen. Mitzi switched her lamp on in a panic.

'Mitzi!' protested Dilly, shielding her eyes.

Mitzi was out of bed, scrambling around the floor on all fours.

'There she is!'

Mitzi had found Lily under the bed. 'There you are!' she cried.

'You must have kicked her out of bed when you were dreaming,' said Dilly, yawning. 'Now, can we go back to sleep please?'

Mitzi struggled to get Lily out from under the bed.

'Dilly,' she said, in her sweetest voice. 'Can you help me please? Lily's very heavy.'

Dilly sighed, and just to be sure that Mitzi understood how fed up she was, she sighed again. But she got out of bed, and together they heaved Lily up onto Mitzi's bed.

There were no more alarms that night, and Lily was lying peacefully beside Mitzi when she woke up. She gave Lily an extra-special cuddle, and a kiss. Dilly, who had also just woken up, rolled her eyes and went to the bathroom.

'Now you lie there, while Mama goes to the bathroom to have a wee-wee, then I'll go and have some breakfast, and then we'll go out, OK?'

'Drink, Mama?'

'You want a drink?' Mitzi remembered that Baby Cries dolls could 'drink' water and then they would cry and wet their nappies!

'Mama, will get you water. Now you wait there.' Mitzi marched into the bathroom to get a tooth glass and some water.

'Hey!' complained Dilly, who was showering.

'It's all right, Lily wantth a glass of water,' said Mitzi calmly.

'Did it have to be *now*?' asked Dilly.

'Yeth, she said, "Drink Mama".'

Mitzi left, carefully carrying the glass of water.

Dilly and Mitzi shared a bathroom, which was along their corridor – and up two steps – on the third floor of their rambling farmhouse. Ingrid had her own bedroom on the first floor, with a 'Jack and Jill' bathroom, which she shared with Ruby. The two boys shared a bedroom, and they had a bathroom on the second floor, and their parents had their own en-suite bathroom. The two boys were the only children to have a bath, and so their bathroom was popular! They had recently started a scheme that if one of the girls wanted a bath, they had to pay the boys something, either in money or by doing some of the boys' chores. The girls complained, but their parents told them to work things out themselves, so they did.

Mitzi returned to the bedroom with the glass of water and held it up to Lily's mouth. She poured it in sip by sip, taking tender care with it.

'Say ta, Mama,' said Mitzi.

'Ta, Mama.'

'That'th right. Good girl.' And with that, she went down to breakfast.

The family always ate together unless Dad was at a vital point in one of his stories. Today everyone was sitting around the large kitchen table when Mitzi piped up.

'Mummy, can I get some clothes for Lily?'

'You're really taken with that dolly, aren't you?' Mum appeared to think for a moment. 'All right, come with me after breakfast, Mitzi, I think I might still have some of your clothes from when you were small.'

'She's still small,' said Oscar with a snigger, which of course set Jacky off as well. The two boys snorted over their bacon and eggs.

'*Smaller*, then. You two were smaller than Mitzi at her age, you know. Now eat sensibly please you two.' That shut them up! They concentrated on their food.

– CHAPTER FOUR–

OH, WHERE HAS MY LILY DOLL GONE?

Sure enough, after breakfast, Mum took Mitzi to a cupboard that the children called the lumber room. It was high up under the roof of the house. Mum pulled open a drawer.

'Yes, there they are,' she said. 'These are your things from when you were about two and three. I was going to give them to charity, but I hadn't got around to it yet, with all the lockdown and everything. They should fit your dolly nicely.'

Mitzi carried her old clothes proudly back to her bedroom, where she stood and stared in horror. There was no sign of Lily. Her precious dolly had disappeared! Her first thought was that Jacky and Oscar were to blame. She raced out of her room, down the three flights of stairs in a headlong rush. She burst into the kitchen panting from the running and seething with anger. Her eyes blazed as she faced her older brothers.

'What have you done with her!' she shouted.

'Done with who?' asked Oscar, genuinely puzzled.

'My Lily, my dolly, she's gone!' And she pushed him as hard as she could.

Ingrid, hearing the fuss, paused as she loaded the dishwasher – it should have been Oscar's job, but Ingrid had had a bath the day before. She came over.

'Mitz, Mitz, calm down!' she said. 'Jacky and Oscar have been here all the time. Besides, no one would mess around with your things. Come on, we'll look for her together.'

Once they got upstairs, they roped in Dilly and Ruby. The four girls first searched the bedroom, then extended the search to the rest of the third floor.

'There!' exclaimed Dilly, just as Mitzi was getting frantic. She had found Lily in the bathroom. 'You must have brought her in here and forgotten.'

'I didn't, I didn't!' Mitzi stamped her little foot.

'Maybe she walked into the bathroom by herself!' said Ruby, the mistress of sarcasm.

'It's OK, Mitz,' soothed Ingrid. 'The main thing is, we've found her.'

Mitzi dried her tears. She insisted on carrying Lily by herself – she wouldn't let anyone help – and struggled back to the bedroom. Once there, she closed the bedroom door, shutting everyone out. Her sisters looked at each other, shrugged and got on with what they had been doing before they were interrupted. Ingrid went back to filling the dishwasher. Ruby went back to her room, where she was trying out different hairstyles, and Dilly went back to her chemistry set.

Mitzi, happy to be alone with Lily at last, put a

pillow on the floor to use as a changing mat.

'Here we are, Lily. I've got some nice new clotheth for you. They're not really new, they uthed to be mine, but I'm too big for them now. They'll fit you jutht right. Now let's get this onesie off you. You're a very clever dolly. You can move and drink and talk.'

'I can put my own clothes on too!' said Lily to Mitzi's surprise.

Mitzi started to pull Lily's onesie off. Lily smacked Mitzi's hand away.

'I'll do it, Mama!' she said, with the usual delay in between the phrases. 'You can turn your back, Mama!'

An astonished Mitzi did as she was told. Behind her there was a rustling.

'There's something missing, Mama!' said Lily in a cross tone. Mitzi turned.

A minute or two later a confused Mum followed the sounds of bumps and crashes from upstairs and found Mitzi rootling through the drawers in the lumber room.

'Where are my old pants?' wailed Mitzi. 'Lily hasn't got any pants.'

'Oh dear!' replied Mum, joining in with Mitzi's game. 'We'd better find her some then, hadn't we?' They managed to find several pairs of underwear from one or other of the girls when they were younger.

Mitzi happily trotted off back to her room, where she handed over a pair of pants to Lily. Then she turned her back again. She heard more rustling.

'Ready, Mama,' announced Lily.

Mitzi sat down on the floor to face Lily, who was now dressed in a t-shirt and a pair of dungarees that used to belong to Mitzi. She also had on a pair of trainers that had belonged to Oscar when he was three. They still had his name in them. Even if she was dressed in borrowed clothes, Lily was very much her own person – she was nobody's toy anymore!

– CHAPTER FIVE –
LILY WHO?

As Mitzi sat on the floor opposite Lily, she put things together in her head.

1. She's very heavy, much heavier than my other dollies.
2. She drinks lots of water, but she doesn't cry or wet her nappy – she doesn't even have a nappy!
3. She was under the bed in the night, and she was in the bathroom. She moves by herself!
4. She speaks and answers me.
5. She's not a dolly. She's a real person!'

Mitzi looked Lily directly in the eyes. 'Who are you?' she asked at last.

'I'm a princess,' said Lily. 'My name is Aramantha, and I'm from a world a long way away.'

'Wow,' said Mitzi. 'I'm Mitzi. I'm not a princeth, but Mummy says I'm thpecial.'

'That's what mummies do,' said Aramantha. A tear slid down her cheek, just like Mitzi's other Baby Cries dolls, but this tear was real.

'Where's your mummy?' asked Mitzi.

'At home... back on my world.'

'Where's your daddy?'

More tears fell from Lily's purple eyes. 'I think he might be dead.'

Mitzi was shocked. As far as she was concerned mummies and daddies were there forever. She had a vague idea that at some point they turned into grannies and grandads. She had never considered the idea that they would die one day.

Aramantha went on, 'We were going to visit another planet, to see my...' There was a long pause. 'I think you would call him my fiancé.'

'What's that?' asked Mitzi curiously. 'I don't know that word.'

'Don't you have a fiancé?'

'I don't think so. What does it do?'

That made Aramantha laugh. She stood up, and Mitzi watched in astonishment as Aramantha toddled back and forth. It was the first time she had seen her walk. Aramantha walked perfectly normally over to the box of tissues on the little table by Mitzi's bed, and wiped her eyes. She came back and sat down again.

'Anyway,' she said, 'we were on our way when we were attacked by some bad people who hate my planet, and my fiancé's planet. We crashed here on Earth. My daddy told me to hide. We look like humans, but I'm only small. He told me to find somewhere to hide, so I ran as fast my little legs would carry me. Then I saw the toy shop.'

'Didn't anyone see you?'

'It was your dark period.'

'You mean night-time?'

'Yes, that sounds right to me. There was nobody to see. I saw the dolls in the shop window, and I thought I could hide there for a while. I found a window and climbed in. I took the clothes off one of the dolls. She was big enough for me to fit into them. They were horrible! They itched! I had to sit still for hours, but I couldn't help blinking, and you saw me. I tried to get away, but you found me again!'

'Oh, oh dear. I'm sorry. Should I have left you there?'

'No, it's safer here. Far away from where we crashed. I like it here. I couldn't wait for a drink any longer, so I had to speak. You still thought I was a toy person… a dolly, but I decided I had to trust you. Then I had to, er, to what did you call it? Wee-wee. I couldn't wait. I thought I could get to the waste disposal and back before you came back, but you were too quick!'

'Waste disposal? Oh, you mean the toilet!' Mitzi laughed. Then they were both laughing.

'Toy-let' said Aramantha, practising.

Later, at lunchtime, Ingrid noticed that Mitzi took more sandwiches than usual. When she looked up again, Mitzi's pile of sandwiches had vanished, except the one that Mitzi was holding, just about to take a bite. Ingrid blinked.

'Wow, Mitzi, you must have really gulped those sandwiches down!'

Mitzi blushed, but said nothing.

Mum looked up. 'Don't eat too quickly, dear,' she murmured. 'You don't want to get a tummy ache.'

'No, Mummy. Mummy, whatth a fianthay?'

'A what?'

Dilly, who was good at interpreting Mitzi's lisp, said, 'Do you mean fiancé, Mitzi?'

'Yeth. What's that, and do I have one?'

'Where did you hear that word?' asked Mum.

'Oh,' said Mitzi airily. 'I just heard it somewhere. Is it a bad word?'

'Well, no. It just means the man you are going to marry. He's your boyfriend until he asks you to marry him, then he's your fiancé. It means "promised", as in you are promised to each other in marriage. So no, you haven't got one!'

Mitzi now had a lot to think about and she went quiet. She knew that girls grew into women, and that most women fell in love with men, but she couldn't see why. The only males she knew well were her father and brothers.

I s'pose I could marry daddy. But someone like Oscar or Jacky? Yucky! They're so silly!' Out loud she said, 'I'm never getting married!'

Mum smiled. 'Well, there's no hurry, darling. After all, you're only six, you can't get married until you're eighteen.'

'OK, Mummy. May I get down now?'

'All right, darling. Off you go, I suppose you're going up to play with Lily.'

'Her name's not Lily anymore.'

'Oh? What is it now, then?'

'Itth Aramantha'

'Aramansa?' asked Dilly.

'No, *Aramantha*, I wasn't lithping!'

– CHAPTER SIX –

THE CAT GETS OUT OF THE BAG

Mitzi ran off upstairs. 'Can I get down too, Mummy?' said Ingrid, suddenly in a hurry.

'Yes, darling. Have you done your chores?'

'Ruby's on duty now.' Ruby pulled a face but nodded resignedly.

Ingrid followed Mitzi up the stairs. As quietly as a mouse she sneaked up to the third floor. Mitzi's bedroom door was firmly closed, but like the other doors in the house, it was an old-fashioned one – it had a keyhole.

Ingrid knelt down and peered through it. She could see Mitzi, who had her back to the door. She was playing with her new doll.

'Aha! That's where the sandwiches went.'

She was feeding her with sandwiches she had brought up from downstairs. So far so normal. What she saw next, however, was definitely not normal!

Mitzi moved aside for a moment, and Ingrid could see Lily, no, not Lily. What was it? *Aramantha*! Whatever her name was, she was *eating* the sandwiches! And drinking water from Mitzi's *Bluey* toothbrush mug. The doll was not a doll – it was alive!

Ingrid was astonished, and at the same time frightened. She watched as the so-called doll sat on the bed swinging her legs and chatting pleasantly to her sister. She looked like a little girl of Mitzi's age, but scaled down. She was wearing some of Mitzi's old clothes.

What is she doing in Mitzi's bedroom? Is Mitzi in danger? thought Ingrid, peeking through the keyhole again. Mitzi didn't seem to be in immediate danger. She and Aramantha were conversing in what seemed like a friendly way.

Ingrid crept back downstairs. She went to the quiet room and sat in thought. She would speak to Aramantha and make sure she meant no harm to Mitzi.

Ingrid went back and sat on the third-floor landing and waited.

Sure enough, Mitzi eventually came out of the room to go to the bathroom.

Ingrid slipped into the bedroom. Aramantha was sitting, frozen in her dolly pose.

'You don't have to do that,' said Ingrid. 'I saw you eating sandwiches and talking with Mitzi.'

Aramantha turned her head slowly towards Ingrid and blinked once. Then she abandoned her pose, dusted herself off, and got to her feet.

'I am the princess Aramantha of the Planet Boldera, and I wish to claim asylum,' she said proudly. Ingrid noticed there was a slight delay when Aramantha spoke.

'Um, I'm not an adult, I can't help you, erm, your

royal highness. But if you like I'll speak to Mum and Dad.'

'Who is Mumandad. Is she your chief?'

Ingrid laughed. 'In a way. They're my parents – my mother and my father. Mother is Mum and father is Dad, see?'

'Yes, I see. My mother is the queen, and we live far away. My father, the king, is somewhere here – lost on your world, if he is still alive. Our ship crashed in the hills a little way from the town where you found me. *They* followed us down. They are looking for me. They want to stop the marriage between me and my fiancé.'

Aha! thought Ingrid. *That explains why Mitzi was asking what a fiancé is!*

Aramantha carried on speaking. 'It will bring our planets into a union. That frightens them.'

'Your fiancé? How old are you?'

I am thirty of your Earth years. For us that is the middle of our childhood.'

'That's a long childhood!'

'It enables us to learn everything we need to know about taking a full part in adult life. That is for the ruling classes only, the aristocrats, of course. For the lower classes they start working much earlier. Are you an aristocrat here on your planet?'

Ingrid laughed. 'An aristocrat? No. I'm eleven years old and my name is Ingrid. I will be going away to school soon.'

'School?' Aramantha cocked her head on one side for a moment, then said, 'Ah yes, school. A learning place, where your children are taught basic knowledge. I have what you would call private tutors. You are only eleven years? In height and development, you look to me like one of our fifty-year-olds. When I am fifty, I will be as tall as you.'

'To me you look about three years old.'

'I was barely out of the egg when I was three!'

'The egg?'

Before Aramantha could reply, Mitzi exploded into the room, threw herself on the bed and swept the princess into an embrace.

'Aramantha'th *my* friend!' she wailed.

Ingrid sat next to her. 'Mitz, I just wanted to be sure you were safe. Mummy's told you about stranger danger, hasn't she!'

'Aramantha wouldn't hurt me, would you?'

'No, but there are people after me and they are very dangerous people, Mitzi. They might hurt you to get to me. I need to find my father – if he is still alive. He sent a distress call. Our people will come. Then I must go to meet my fiancé.'

'I don't want you to go,' sniffed Mitzi.

'One day soon, I must go, Mitzi, but you and I have bonded, and we will always remember each other.' With that Aramantha pulled Mitzi to her and touched foreheads with her. 'Anyway,' she added. 'I am not going just yet!'

'Where would your father go?' asked Ingrid. 'If he survived the crash?'

Aramantha's head drooped, and she pulled a sad

face. 'I don't know. I was put into a… I think you call it a lifeboat. I have my tracker. He will find me, or one of our servants will.'

'Whatth a tracker?' asked Mitzi

'A device implanted into my head. It connects me with the computer on the ship, and that enables me to speak your language. You may have noticed there is a delay when I speak. Well, the computer is sending me messages, helping me to translate what you say, and it tells me what to reply. It also means that my people can track me. The ship can't be totally destroyed. The computer must still be working because I can understand you. I need to claim asylum – here – in your house.'

Mitzi looked at Ingrid. Ingrid thought hard.

'I think it's best if we keep this a secret between us kids for now, Mitzi. I'll tell Mummy and Daddy if I have to, but I won't if I can avoid it.'

'What are we going to do?'

Ingrid knew that Mitzi trusted her completely.

'I'll think of something!' declared Ingrid.

– CHAPTER SEVEN –

THE SEARCH BEGINS

Ingrid decided that the search for the missing spaceship and Aramantha's father should begin close to where Aramantha was found in Kendal, but they couldn't all troop off to Kendal on their own. Apart from anything else, they had no way of getting there. So, Ingrid put on her thinking cap. After thinking for some time, she went in search of her mother.

'Mummy,' she said in honeyed tones. 'I need a phone case to keep my lovely new phone all nice and safe, and Mitzi would like to get some more things for Aramantha. Can we go into Kendal again soon?'

'What is it you still need? Can't we get it online?'

'Oh, um, I'd rather get it from the shops in Kendal. I'll do it myself. If you take me there, I'll go into the shops while you take Mitzi to the toyshop. I've saved some money and I would like to treat her to a new toy.

Her mother thought.

'Well, you're a big girl now, so I suppose I can trust you to buy things from the shop. All right, we'll go into Kendal. You know I like shopping anyway, almost as much as your father does! When do you want to go?'

'Tomorrow?'

'OK, fine, I'll tell Daddy. He can keep an eye on the boys and Dilly and Ruby.'

Part one of operation "F.A.D" (find Aramantha's daddy) had begun.

The next day, Mitzi dressed in her nicest clothes. She was on her best behaviour as the three of them made their way out to the car. Ingrid was in her smarter jeans and a nice t-shirt. It was a hot day, and Ingrid panted as she walked to the car with her biggest rucksack on her back. The most uncomfortable one, however, was Aramantha, who was hiding in the rucksack! Mitzi sat in her child seat in the front, next to her mother. Ingrid sat in the seat behind her mother, and discreetly opened the flap of her rucksack, which was on the floor between her legs, and peeped in. A red sweaty face looked up at her.

'Erm, is the air conditioning on, Mummy?' Ingrid asked, as they drove along.

'You'll feel it soon, dear,' said Mum.

'Good,' said Ingrid, and she smiled at the princess's perspiring face.

What a way to treat royalty! Ingrid thought.

After what seemed an age, they reached the town. The air conditioning had worked nicely, and Aramantha's face looked quite a bit cooler as they turned into the car park in Kendal town centre. Ingrid closed the flap on her backpack and heaved it onto her back. She parted company with her mother and Mitzi and headed off towards the clothes shop.

*

Laura watched her go with a smile of pride. *Fancy giving her precious pocket money to Mitzi so she could buy some toys. Ingrid is really growing up into a nice, kind young woman!'* she thought fondly. 'Come on, Mitzi,' she said. 'We'll find some nice things. How about a new tea service for your dollies?'

Ingrid went into the department store in the Westmorland Shopping Centre, straight through without even glancing at the perfumes, make-up, or clothes, and emerged from a door at the side of the store in Blackhall Road.

'Can you hear me all right, Aramantha?' Ingrid said, panting.

'Yes, keep talking! As we get closer to the ship the translator signal from the computer gets stronger. I think we are quite close now.'

Ingrid followed Aramantha's directions, reciting speeches she could remember from her Shakespeare lessons: poems, songs, anything. She did get some strange looks as she passed people in the street though!

They went on, turning left onto Stramongate, and towards the river. As they crossed the bridge, Ingrid was reciting 'When I was one I had just begun…' when Aramantha said, 'Stop, Ingrid. Go back.'

Ingrid obeyed.

'The ship is here!'

'Where?' said Ingrid, looking around in puzzlement. There was no sign of a spaceship. 'Oh, wait. Is it invisible?'

'No. We don't have a… I think you call it a "cloaking

device".'

Ingrid nodded, the spaceships in Daddy's stories sometimes had such a device, which made them invisible to other ships.

'Aramantha, er, your royal highness, I'm going to have to put you down. This bag is so heavy.' She placed the rucksack on the floor and spoke into it. One lady came up to her.

'Are you all right, dear?' she asked.

Ingrid blushed. 'Um, yes, I'm, er, I'm rehearsing for the school play, going over my lines…'

The lady smiled. 'I see,' she said, and she walked on.

'So where is the ship? I can't see it,' she said with a hiss.

'I think it's underneath us.'

'What? In the river? It crashed in the river?'

Aramantha, of course could not see anything from inside the bag. 'We're over a river? I thought I could hear water! Yes. Yes, that's a good place to hide. Take me down to the riverbank.'

Ingrid grabbed her rucksack and swung it once more onto her poor aching shoulders. She took Aramantha under the bridge and down to the water's edge.

'Can you see anything?' came Aramantha's voice from the bag.

Ingrid squinted down into the water. It was quite deep at this point, where the fast-moving river Kent had dug itself a channel.

'Maybe,' she said doubtfully, peering into the water in the shadows under the bridge. 'I think there might be something made of grey metal down there. It doesn't look big enough to be a spaceship. I think it's just a bit of old metal.

'Let me out,' commanded Aramantha.

Ingrid was getting just a little fed up with these orders from Aramantha. Princess or not she was the size of a small child – a bad-mannered small child! Even Mitzi knew how to say 'please' and 'thank you'.

As she squinted into the six-foot deep water, Ingrid couldn't help but smile as she remembered Mitzi's first attempts, when she was around fifteen months old.

'Peas, Ingwid, 'Kyou, Ingwid.'

Their mother had winked and remarked, 'Now you know where we get the saying "mind your p's and q's", Ingrid... It's toddler-speak for "please and thank you!"'

Ingrid returned to the present. 'Would it kill you to say please and thank you now and then?' she murmured to Aramantha.

Aramantha looked surprised. 'Oh,' she mused. 'Please and thank you? I don't think Bolderan princesses say please and thank you.'

'Well, you're not on Boldera now it's...' Ingrid racked her brains for the right phrase. 'It's culturally appropriate,' she said at last. 'For our culture. It will get you on quicker here.'

'Very well. Then thank you, let me out, Ingrid, I'm boiling hot.' Ingrid let her out of the rucksack.

'Please,' said the princess.

Oh well, I suppose she is at least trying, Ingrid thought, and she gave the princess a little smile.

On the deserted riverbank, underneath the bridge,

away from prying eyes, the two girls, one human and one Bolderan, knelt and peered into the river.

'I see it!' exclaimed Aramantha. Before Ingrid knew what was happening, Aramantha had jumped fully clothed into the water. She plunged in and dived beneath the surface. Ingrid could see her swimming strongly towards the mystery object.

Aramantha was back in a millisecond. She put a small object, about the size and shape of an ostrich egg, onto the riverbank. The 'egg' was made of a shiny metal. Ingrid pulled her out of the water. She was dripping wet.

'It's a locator,' Aramantha announced, showing Ingrid the device.

'A what?'

'A locator. A… beacon. I had to get close up before I could see what it was. You were right, it isn't a spaceship, but my implant connected with it. It has given me the co-ordinates of the ship. It's close by.' She stopped, her head on one side as if she was listening to something.

There was a long pause, then Aramantha recited in a sing-song voice: '54/21/30 North by 2/56/10 West. It is about seven of your miles away. Is that a long way to walk?'

'Too long!' replied Ingrid. 'We have to go back now. Mummy will be wondering where I am. We'll look up those co-ordinates on my computer tonight, and see where they lead, then maybe we'll have a family outing!'

– CHAPTER EIGHT –

THE SEARCH CONTINUES

Ingrid went back into the shop through the side entrance. Remembering why she was officially there, she bought a nice phone case. She also bought some spare PE kit plus some replacements for clothes she had grown out of. Luckily, there wasn't a queue. She hurried back to the car with her purchases.

Mum and Mitzi were sitting in the car. Mitzi was examining her lovely new dolls' tea service, bought with the generous donation from her sister's pocket money.

'I was getting a bit worried,' said Mum.

'Sorry, Mummy. There were queues everywhere,' said Ingrid. She couldn't help but blush at this little white lie.

'Did you get everything?'

'Yes, thank you, Mum. I had a good look round, too.'

'I should think you did!'

They set off for home. After a few minutes there came a little 'achoo!' from the back of the car.

'Are you all right, Ingrid?'

'Erm, just a little sneeze, mum. I think you can turn off the air conditioning now.'

'I hope that's not COVID. I can't face being stuck in the house again.'

Oh, neither can I! thought Ingrid. 'I'm sure I'm fine, Mum,' she said. *But I can't speak for Aramantha. An alien princess with a virus? That's all we need!*

Once they arrived back home, Ingrid hurried upstairs as fast as she could go with the heavy bag on her back. She helped Aramantha out of the bag, then ushered her into the bathroom. She helped the Bolderan to take off her clothes, and Aramantha dried herself thoroughly with handtowels, then wrapped them round her. Ingrid put the wet clothes on a towel on Mitzi's bed. And used the hair dryer to dry them.

Ingrid's own new clothes were tightly wrapped in a polythene bag, so they had escaped being soaked by a wet princess. Ingrid went down to show them to Mum and Dilly. She took her time over this. She did not want Dilly to go up to the bedroom and walk in on Aramantha! Ruby was there too, and was happy to give her opinion on the new clothes and phone cover. Which was, mainly 'Cool phone cover, but boring clothes. But I suppose you have to be boring at school!'

Ingrid finished showing off her purchases and put them away in her bedroom. After that, she spent some time on her computer. Then she went back up to the next floor and found Aramantha, fully dressed, on the bed, sitting with Mitzi.

Ingrid closed the door. 'I looked up those co-ordinates on the Internet,' she said. They're in lake Windermere. It looks like your spaceship really is underwater after all,

Aramantha.'

'That's good news, Ingrid. You are a good help. I shall make you a… the computer is having difficulty with the translation… a knight counsellor of Boldera… it's a particularly important position.'

'Um, thank you, er, your royal highness, but we still need to work out how to get you to Windermere.'

She left Mitzi and Aramantha in the bedroom. As she left, Mitzi was showing the alien girl her brand-new dolly's tea set. Ingrid smiled to see that Aramantha was being polite about it.

Captain Ingrid now realised she was going to have to tell her commando troop about Aramantha and explain their new mission: to reunite the princess with her spaceship – and hopefully with her father, the king, too.

She went into the living room, where her mother was helping Dilly with some of her scientific experiments.

'Erm, hi, Mum.'

Mum looked up. 'Whenever you use that tone of voice, Ingrid, you make me nervous! You have something on your mind! What is it?'

'Well, now that the school holidays are here, and the weather looks so nice, I wondered if it might be nice to have a family outing tomorrow.'

'But, Ingrid, you've just had an outing.'

'Yes, but all of us. I thought we might go to Windermere. Have ice cream and fish and chips, like we used to?'

'Ah,' said Mum. 'I get it. Now you're about to go away to school – if we ever get out of this lockdown that is – you're feeling nostalgic for this chaotic family of ours!'

'Um, I guess…'

'All right, why not. We'll all go. I'll see if Daddy can tear himself away from his writing, and we'll have a family trip.'

Ingrid smiled with relief. She went over and hugged her mother.

'Thanks, Mummy.'

With a light heart she skipped back upstairs to tell Aramantha the good news.

Later that evening, when their parents were busy, Ingrid called a meeting of the clan. Everyone was duly astonished when she and Mitzi revealed that Aramantha was not a doll at all but a real live princess from a different planet. The princess basked in all the attention and seemed to enjoy being called 'your highness' by everyone.

'Right,' ordered Captain Ingrid of the 5th Yorkshire commandos. She used the blackboard from Jacky and Oscar's bedroom to illustrate her points.

'This is top secret, right? Tomorrow we are going to Windermere, where we think Aramantha's spaceship is. When we get there we will go for a row on the lake, and she will search for the ship. She can detect it with the tracker in her head. When she has pinpointed its location, she will swim down to the ship. She can hold her breath for a long time. She can get in through the airlock and see if there is anyone in there still alive. Now, this is the plan…'

– CHAPTER NINE –

FOUND!

The next day, the family set off with a light heart for Lake Windermere. The car was packed with Chans, the boot was full of picnic – scrumptious food and drink – and Ingrid's rucksack was the temporary home for the Bolderan princess.

The fifty-mile trip to Windermere passed quickly enough, with everyone on their gaming devices or chatting. Ruby was listening to her favourite singer on her headphones. Dad had to remind her that her headphones didn't stop the rest of the car from hearing her out-of-tune singing! She sulked for a while, but she perked up when they got to the lake.

At this time, in spite of the lockdown, people were allowed to gather outside if they were in the same family group, but not otherwise. Nonetheless, the fine weather had brought out a good many people.

'There's a parking space, darling,' said Dad. Mum parked the car at the small Beech Hill car park. It was usually a bit quieter than the other car parks, as it had steep steps to get to the lakeside, which not everyone liked. Mum insisted that they had their lunch in the picnic area together, before splitting up into different activities.

'Now,' she said, as they were all finishing up their lunch. 'What are you all planning? I'm sure you've been planning something, haven't you?' The children looked at each other.

Oscar was in the middle of his favourite roll. 'Um, me and Jackie and Dilly thought we would go swimming in the lake,' he said through his mouthful of bread, cheese, and onion.

'Don't talk with your mouth full, dear. In that case Daddy will come with you. You know he enjoys his wild swimming.' She looked pointedly at Ingrid. 'And you, Ingrid?'

'Um, Ruby and I thought we'd take Mitzi on the lake in a rowing boat. She's never been in a boat.'

Mum looked at Ingrid for some time. 'Are you sure you can stay safe, and keep Mitzi safe?'

'You taught us, Mum!' said Ingrid.

'All right, but stay close… where I can see you, don't go too far out. Remember you have to have enough strength to row back!'

'I know, Mum,' said Ingrid.

'Right, come on then, everyone, help me clear up the picnic, then we'll go down to the shore.'

Ingrid looked around. So far everyone was playing their part. The plan was working!

Everyone pitched in and the picnic was soon cleared away, leaving not a trace to spoil the beauty spot.

Dad and the boys changed into their swimming things in the toilets and walked down to the lakeshore in their trunks, trainers, and beach robes.

Ingrid held Mitzi's hand as they walked down the one hundred and eleven steps to the stony beach.

What would happen if I fell now? Ingrid thought. *And hurt Aramantha? It would probably start an interplanetary war!*

She took extra care and held Mitzi's hand tightly!

'Ow, you're squishing me!'

'Sorry, Mitzi.'

People going scuba diving often based themselves on the stony little beach at the bottom of the steps, but when the Chans got down there, there was no one else around. They had the place to themselves.

That's lucky, thought Ingrid.

To Ingrid's chagrin, Mum decided to walk along with the girls as they strolled around the shore to the boat-hire jetty – that wasn't part of the plan. Ingrid approached the young woman in charge of the boats. She was wearing a mask, even though they were outside.

'Erm, how much to take a rowing boat out please?' she asked.

The woman looked at her.

'How old are you, sweetheart?' she asked.

Ingrid blushed. 'Twelve…' She looked at her mother, '…nearly.'

'So, you're eleven.'

'Um. Yes.'

'Is that a problem?' inquired Mum.

'You have to be fourteen, or you have to have an adult with you.'

'Well, that's all right, Ingrid. I'll come with you. I can

sit quietly and read my e-reader while you row me along the lake. It'll be lovely.'

Oh no! The plan was in ruins! Ingrid could see no way out. She looked helplessly at her siblings, who looked helplessly back. She knew they were trusting Captain Ingrid to come up with something, but she had nothing! There was only one thing for it…plan B. Full disclosure!

'Um, that will be lovely, Mum,' said Ingrid with a gulp. 'But when we get in the boat, Mum, there's something I need to tell you.'

The boat was £27.50 per hour. Mum paid a deposit and they loaded the boat with rucksacks and a couple of nice warm blankets – it might be chilly out on the lake. Then they were off. Ingrid rowed the four Chans – and one stowaway – out far enough so that they would not be overheard.

'It's like this, Mum… um…'

'Is this something to do with Mitzi's new dolly?' asked Mum.

The three girls stared at her, speechless with surprise.

'Oh, come on. You all seem to have got caught up in this, whatever it is. The only thing I've heard from any of you recently is about Mitzi's dolly, Lily. How we have to get clothes for Lily and how Lily needs a dolly's tea set, and suddenly we all have to go chasing around the countryside. First, Ingrid has to buy some more new things in Kendal, then we have to come to Windermere. I'm exhausted with all this activity! Just what is going on?'

Ingrid did not know what to say. After opening and shutting her mouth helplessly for a few moments, she shrugged her shoulders and opened her rucksack. Aramantha climbed out and stood up, full of dignity.

'I am princess Aramantha, of the thirty-fifth generation of the royal house of Martanum, heir to the throne of Boldera. Under interplanetary law and custom, I claim asylum on your planet.'

Mum sat for a moment, then burst out laughing. 'How clever!' she exclaimed. 'Just like Buzz Lightyear!' She smiled at Aramantha. 'To infinity and beyond!' She laughed.

The girls looked at her horrified.

'What? Wait… You mean this is real? I mean, *she* is real?' She stared at Aramantha, who calmly gazed back.

'I thought she was just an awfully expensive, very clever talking dolly. I assumed you had got away with paying too little money, and that now you were worried about it. I thought that was what all the secrecy was about!'

'No, Mum,' said Ingrid. 'Princess Aramantha is real. She's looking for her spaceship. Her father put her into an escape pod when they were attacked. The ship crashed in the water somewhere near here. Aramantha can locate it. We don't know if there is anyone alive down there, but we know the ship's computer is still working.'

'Oh, matriarch of the family Chan,' spoke Aramantha, using her best, most formal speech. 'I beseech your help in this matter.'

Mum was still struggling not to laugh, but she bit her lip, and tried to match the dignity of the little princess. 'But how, ahem, how will we find the spaceship if it's under the water, it gets very deep here – up to 200 feet, I think.'

'Aramantha has an implant, Mum,' said Ingrid. 'She uses it like a sort of compass, or a radio direction finder.'

Aramantha held up her hand for silence. She cocked her head on one side as if listening. 'We are very close now,' she said excitedly. Then, without a further word, to Mum's astonishment and alarm, Aramantha leapt over the side of the boat and disappeared into Windermere's murky depths.

Mum was so shocked that she couldn't speak for a moment, then she gasped out, 'Oh my…' She stood up in the boat and started to take her coat off. The boat rocked dangerously from side to side.

'No, Mum, wait, she's fine. She can hold her breath a really long time, and she swims like a fish,' said Ingrid, desperately pulling her mother back down onto the seat. Mum sat back down and Ingrid breathed a sigh of relief as the boat stopped its dangerous pitching up and down.

'Are you sure she's all right?'

'Quite sure, Mum,' blustered Ingrid, who wasn't really sure. She bit her lip as time passed and there was no sign of Aramantha. They all stared down into the water.

'Ingrid, I really think we should get some help,' said Mum. 'She's been down there an awfully long—'

She stopped as she was interrupted by a jubilant little figure, erupting from the water. Willing hands pulled her back on board. Aramantha stood there, dripping wet, and making a big puddle in the bottom of the boat.

– CHAPTER TEN –

STAND BY TO WAIT!

Aramantha playfully spurted water into Ruby's face. 'My father, the king, and some of his engineers survived the crash,' she said. 'They are trying to mend the damage. He was so pleased to see me!' She laughed out loud, and everyone laughed with her, except the soaking wet Ruby, who crossly wiped her face with one of the blankets. Mitzi snatched the blanket and wrapped it round Aramantha to keep her warm.

'Come on, lieutenant,' ordered Captain Ingrid and she and Ruby pulled for the shore.

'He said to go back to your house and wait there. The ship is almost ready, but I fear our enemies are just waiting for us, hiding somewhere in your solar system.'

Ingrid opened her rucksack, and Aramantha climbed wearily in. It had been a long swim, even for her and she was tired now.

'We will sleep!' she said. Every inch, all twenty-four of them, a princess.

'Do the others know about, er, Aram, Antham, er, the princess?' asked Mum.

'Yes, except Daddy,' said Ruby. 'Can *I* tell him?'

Mum looked at Mitzi and Ingrid in turn. Ruby was not the best one at telling a story, she often got mixed up and confused, which made it hard to follow her. Ingrid shrugged and Mitzi was busy settling Aramantha comfortably into the backpack.

'All right, Ruby. But maybe rehearse what you are going to say in your head. That way, you'll get the story clear!'

Ruby gave an exaggerated TUT! (But she rehearsed what she was going to say anyway.)

They finally got back to the landing. The teenager in charge of the boats said, 'That was quick!'

Ingrid couldn't resist a joke. She said, 'Something came up!' That made everyone snort with laughter. The boat-hire person looked at them in confusion, but they told her nothing.

'Well, it's still £27.50, even though you only had half an hour,' she said grumpily.

There were more people about now and Ingrid took good care to make sure the flap on her rucksack was shut as they walked back to the stony beach.

When they got there, there was no sign of the others at first, then Mitzi spotted them in the water about forty-five metres out from the shore. The three girls all waved and shouted. Dad and the boys, with Dilly, raced each other back to the shore. Dilly won, as always. She was laughing and panting as she took off her swimming goggles and grabbed her towel.

'All right?' she hissed at Ingrid.

Ingrid shook her head. 'Kind of. We had to tell Mum.

They wouldn't let us out on the boat on our own. Mum's cool. Aramantha found the spaceship all right. But she's coming back home with us.'

'Yay!' said Dilly.

Dad emerged from the water, laughing and wrestling with Oscar and Jacky.

'Hi, Dad,' said Ruby. He looked up and smiled at her.

'Hi, Rubes,' he said.

'Um, Dad, we have a surprise for you. Ingrid has a princess in her rucksack!'

'What?' He laughed thinking his second daughter was joking, which was unusual, it had to be said. 'Don't tell me. Mitzi's Baby Cries doll is a princess doll now!' And he shook his wet hands at her, giving her a second wetting of the day. Mum took over.

'Ruby has gone for dramatic effect over content as usual! Our Eldest and youngest daughters have found an alien, Des.'

'Another one?' He spoke light-heartedly. He still thought they were joking!

'Yes, dear. Another one! Mitzi found her in the toyshop, pretending to be a dolly, and brought her home.'

'Oh, I get it,' said Dad with a smile.

'I don't think you do, Des. This is not a joke! Her name is—'

'Aramantha, Dad,' interrupted Ingrid.

'No! Let me, let me!' cried Ruby. 'Dad, she's a real princess. Her ship crashed in Windermere, but she escaped. She's smaller than Mitzi, but she's not a doll. She walks and talks and everything,' said Ruby, panting.

Dad took some convincing, especially since Aramantha had snuggled down inside the bag, and was fast asleep! But they showed her to him, anyway.

'Her enemies are looking for her.' Ingrid put in. 'We can keep her at our house until the spaceship is fixed and they can take her off to her wedding.'

'Wedding? She's smaller than Mitzi!'

'Yeth. But she hath a fianthay. She hath to marry him, then they both go home to grow up. They grow really tall, like Mummy,' piped up Mitzi.

'It's true, darling. It's August, not April the first! The children have all been keeping the secret, until they could burst.'

Between them they managed to half-convince Dad that what they said was true.

'You can meet her when she's had a sleep,' said Ingrid.

– CHAPTER ELEVEN –

ARAMANTHA LETS HER HAIR DOWN

The next morning, the Chans and Aramantha sat around the kitchen table. Aramantha had to use Mitzi's old highchair. She sat on it as if it were a throne.

'So, what's the plan, your highness?' asked Dad.

'We need to wait until my father comes for me. It will not be long now. A day or two, no more.'

'So, until then we just behave normally.'

'Mum, we're in a lockdown. How do we behave normally?' sarked Ruby.

'Normally for the lockdown. You know what I mean.'

'I'll show Aramantha all my hiding platheth,' said Mitzi.

'I suppose she'll be able to get in there. She's even smaller than you,' said Jacky. Oscar laughed.

'Exthactly,' said Mitzi.

The family went about their business. It was the start of the school holidays (which Mum and Dad always kept to) so no school. Dad went back to his computer and his writing, Mum went back to her easel, and paints. She was doing an illustration for the cover of Dad's latest book. She did illustrations for various authors, but it must be said, she worked just a bit harder and more carefully when it was for Dad's books!

Ingrid took Aramantha and Mitzi into the quiet room. She read to them from the big old Grimms' fairy tales book.

Aramantha was intrigued by the story of *Sleeping Beauty*.

'I sleep a lot,' she said. 'But I've never slept for a hundred years! And how can she marry someone who she just met, like that?'

'It happens a lot in fairy stories,' remarked Ingrid. 'I haven't thought about it before, but it happens in *Cinderella* too, and *Snow White*.'

'And *The Little Mermaid*,' piped up Mitzi.

'I have known my fiancé for some years. We have spent time together. He was chosen by my parents, who know the family. It is an exceptionally good family, with a good pedigree.'

'That makes you sound like a dog, or a horse!' exclaimed Ingrid. 'Don't you get to choose?'

'No,' said Aramantha. 'Choose my own husband? But I might choose the wrong man. That would not be good. No, my parents know best. And it's the best thing for our two planets. Together we are stronger.'

Ingrid sat quiet for a while, thinking.

'Read a story where the girl doethnt have to get married to anybody!' said Mitzi.

Ingrid thought a bit, then she turned to the right page and began, 'Once upon a time, there was a little girl who lived in a village near the forest. Whenever she went out, the little girl wore a red riding cloak, so everyone in the village called her "Little Red Riding Hood"…'

In the living room, Laura and Desmond were having a coffee and a conference.

'I hate it when you bring your work home!' joked Laura.

'Literally, in this case! Though none of us knew that Mitzi's 'dolly' was really an alien when we came back from Kendal. It must have been difficult for her to keep up that pose.'

'It all broke down when Mitzi wanted to undress her and put her in some proper clothes. She was much too royal to allow that!'

'I suppose we can only wait until they come to get her. It'll be a wrench for the children. She's a cute little thing.'

'Apparently she's thirty years old! They keep growing until they reach about sixty, when they are thought of as grown up. The adults are as tall as human adults. They look just like us too. She knows no fear, you know, Des. She dived into the lake without knowing exactly where her spaceship was. She must be able to hold her breath for a long time. She really worried me.'

After lunch, the children took the princess outside and the boys showed her their rolling games. Then they played French cricket. The tennis racquet was as big as

Aramantha. But she was fast and strong once she got the idea of the game. Dilly had a rival for once!

'I like this... playing.'

'I don't suppose you have much fun, do you?' asked Ingrid wisely.

'Yes... fun. I like this fun! Ingrid you will come back with me as my knight counsellor and teach my court how to have fun!'

Ingrid laughed.

'You will have to teach them yourself, Aramantha, I mean, your highness.'

'Aramantha is fine here. It is culturally appropriate,' said Aramantha.

– CHAPTER TWELVE –

THE KNOCK AT THE DOOR

The Dales were utterly quiet. Nobody expected the knock to come in the middle of that night when everyone was asleep. Even the wind was taking a rest. The only sounds were the occasional bark of lonely foxes looking for a mate, and the hooting of owls to warn off feathered intruders, before they launched themselves upon their unsuspecting prey on deathly silent wings.

Bang, bang, BANG! came the knock at the front door of the Chan family's farmhouse. Mitzi had been having her running away dream again and opened her eyes in a daze. Aramantha was lying in a cot next to Mitzi's bed. The cot was last used by Mitzi when she was a toddler. Aramantha's eyes opened wide in fright. She was instantly wide awake.

'Mitzi Chan!' she cried out. 'My implant tells me my father is still with the ship. Our enemies are upon us!'

Mitzi climbed out of bed and shook Dilly.

'Dilly, Dilly,' she said with a hiss. 'Mantha says thith is not her father at the door. What do we do? Oh, wake up, Dilly!'

*

Downstairs, Desmond was making his sleepy way to the door when there came another rat-a-tat-tat.

'I'm coming!' he called. Laura was coming along behind him. She stood on the stairs fastening her dressing gown as her husband opened the door. She could just about make out three figures waiting outside.

There were some sounds, which might have been speech, but it didn't have any words that Laura knew – and she spoke six languages. In fact, there were sounds that didn't sound like any speech in any language she had ever heard. She joined her husband at the door. The three figures looked vaguely human, but not as human as the princess. They had long, thin heads, their eyes were almond shaped, and they were all dressed in long grey robes, like a group of college professors, or a collection of the clergy. The one who seemed to be in charge held up a device. Laura took a step back, thinking it might be a weapon, but then the device spoke, in a mechanical sort of voice. It translated what the aliens had just said.

'Greetings. We have come for the princess.'

'Oh, yes. All right,' said Desmond. 'Come in.'

More alien speech, the translator: 'We will enter. Bring her to us.'

Dilly appeared at the top of the stairs. 'What's happening, Mum?' she asked, sleepily.

'Aramantha's father has come for her, dear.'

'Oh, OK. Maybe they would like to sit down while she gets ready. Erm, maybe have a drink or something to eat? She has to, er, to pack.'

'Something to drink?' said Laura.

'Yes, Mum. Or something to eat, maybe?'

Desmond frowned. 'I think they are in a hurry, Dilly, they want to see Aramantha. He's her father after all.'

'Which one is her father?'

'Oh, well, that one seems to be in charge, so I suppose he is.'

'I see. No, there is really no hurry, Dad. Let them have some wine. You've got all that apple wine you made last year.'

'But, Dilly, time might be important.'

Dilly was growing desperate now.

'Yes,' she hissed. 'Time is especially important. Time is the important word. There is plenty of time to have some wine.'

Laura put a hand on Desmond's arm.

'I think, Aramantha *needs time,* Desmond… to, um, to get ready.'

'Yes!' exclaimed Dilly with relief. 'Yes, that's it. She needs time! OK?' She turned and ran back upstairs.

Desmond shrugged. He and Laura took the aliens through to the large kitchen-diner and sat them down around the big old-fashioned table. Desmond went into the cupboard and brought out several bottes of his apple wine, which was fizzy like champagne. He opened one with a loud POP! Which made all the aliens jump up in fright.

'It's all right,' said Laura. 'It's not dangerous I'll show you.' She poured a glass of the sparkling wine and drank some. She poured more glasses for the 'guests' and encouraged them to drink. All the time she spoke, one of the aliens was pointing the translation device towards her, then they all listened to the alien-speak.

Laura said: 'Drink, drink. Apples are, erm… healthy.'

One of the aliens looked at his glass and said something. The other two looked at theirs. All three sniffed their drinks, then recoiled as the bubbles tickled their faces. One of the aliens made a sound that might have been a laugh. Then they all drank the wine down in one go. Desmond stared, shocked at the way these aliens were treating his carefully brewed apple wine.

'Erm, more?' Laura asked.

They held out their glasses for more of the potent drink. After two bottles of strong wine between the three of them, they began to slow down. The laughing sound began to be heard more and more, and they stopped using the translator, and just talked amongst themselves. They seemed to be having a good time. Laura signalled Desmond to stay where he was, and she crept out to consult with her children.

Ingrid and Dilly were in Dilly's bedroom. The two girls jumped up when the door opened but sagged with relief when they saw it was only their mum.

'OK, you two. We gave you time. What's going on?'

'That's not Aramantha's father. When they knocked, she checked that implant thing. Her father is still with his ship.'

Laura looked around, confused. 'Where is Aramantha, anyway? And where is Mitzi?'

'They climbed out of the window and went to hide in one of Mitzi's hiding places.'

'Mitzi's out there?' Laura waved vaguely in the direction of outside.

'Yes, but she knows what she's doing, Mum. She knows how to hide. What's happening downstairs?'

'Daddy is getting them drunk with his apple wine!' Laura said with a smile. 'You should see them getting all chatty, and laughing in their own language.'

'Should we come down?' Ingrid asked.

'No, darling. If Mitzi and Aramantha are safely away, I think we can tell them she's gone and let them search the house if they want.'

'What do you think will happen when they find her gone?'

'I don't know,' replied Laura thoughtfully. 'Look, round up the others, and lock and bolt this door. Don't let anyone come in.'

Laura returned to their 'guests' downstairs. They were on their third bottle now. It seemed to be going down a treat!

One of the aliens approached Desmond and slapped him on the back.

'It looks like you have new best friends, darling!' She said and smiled mischievously.

The alien who slapped Desmond wobbled back to his seat.

Just then one of the three looked up and spoke. He waved impatiently for the translator. It took his colleagues a little time to remember who had it last. When it was finally produced, he spoke into it.

'Gnarsh, argle wiffle!' exclaimed the machine. Laura

and Desmond looked at each other, totally confused. One of the others grabbed the device. This resulted in a heated argument between the three of them. To the amazement of the two humans, they argued loudly and wrestled around for a moment or two, then the second creature got control of the translator, staggering a little as he pulled the thing from his colleague's grasp. He stood up.

'Grarg, gipple, where, muhush princess?'

Laura was having real trouble keeping her laughter in. 'It's the drink!' she squeaked, desperately holding it together by biting her lip. 'They can't hold it. They're not used to it.' She ran out, fearful she could control herself no longer. She went upstairs to tell the girls what was happening. In between giggles she spoke to Ingrid through the locked door.

'Daddy's got them all drunk!' she chuckled. 'I think it will soon be safe for the princess to come back. Do you know where Mitzi took her?'

'No,' said Ingrid, 'but we can contact her any time, Mum.'

Downstairs, Desmond was replying to the aliens remark. 'Erm, yes. She is taking a long time, isn't she?' said Desmond. 'Er, why don't you lie down while you are waiting?' The translator put this into perfect alienese.

The three aliens looked foggily at one another, and the one who seemed to be the head of the bunch – he was having trouble keeping his eyes open – said something, which sounded like it might be 'yes'.

Desmond guided them into the quiet room and got them to lie down on the various sofas and chairs. They fell immediately to sleep. One of them was still cuddling the fifth bottle of wine. Desmond tiptoed out. Laura was in the living room.

'Now what do we do?' he asked.

'We contact the princess.'

'How?'

Laura held up her mobile. 'By phone! How else? E.T. phone home! Or rather Home phone E.T.!'

'Have you been at the wine, too?' asked Desmond.

'I had one glass that's all – all right two glasses. I had to persuade them it was all right to drink, didn't I!' She tapped in a number on her smartphone. 'I must say, it's powerful stuff. I'll never mock you again, I... Hello, darling,' she said into the phone.

'The baddies are all asleep – all fasht, er fast asleep. You can come back.'

'Who did you phone?' Desmond asked, puzzled.

'Mitzi, of course.'

'Mitzi hasn't got a phone.'

'No, but Ingrid has. Mitzi took it with her, Ingrid told me just now.'

In the old badger sett, behind the flowers and brambles Mitzi and Aramantha nestled together. Mitzi rang off the call, put the phone carefully in her jeans pocket, nudged Aramantha and said. 'Come on, 'Mantha. It's safe to go back now.

As Laura hung up, there came another bang, bang, BANG! at the front door.

– CHAPTER THIRTEEN –

KIDNAP!

Desmond went cautiously to the door and opened it. It was another alien. He looked more human. He was tall but also strongly built, like a wrestler or weightlifter.

'Good night and salutations. I have come for Princess Aramantha.'

'Um, won't you come in?' said Desmond. 'Your colleagues are here. Can I offer you a drink?'

Laura was out in the hall. She was phoning Mitzi again.

'Stay where you are, darling. Someone else has come.'

'We know. Itth Aramantha's daddy,' said Mitzi, then she rang off. There was a commotion from upstairs and the sound of a key in a lock and a door opening, then what sounded like a great clap of thunder as Aramantha came crashing down the stairs, followed by the girls of the Chan family.

Aramantha threw herself at the large alien, who picked her up and hugged her for all she was worth.

They spoke rapidly in their language. The king looked up.

'I thank you so much for taking care of my daughter. She tells me that there are enemy soldiers here. How did you overcome them? They carry dangerous weapons. Where are they?'

Desmond led the way to the quiet room, where the fearsome enemy soldiers were sleeping like babies!

'How did you accomplish this?' asked the astonished king.

Laura came up behind him. She was holding an opened bottle and sipping from her third glass of apple wine.

'With this, your majesty! Can I offer you a glass?'

And she giggled, then burped. 'Oops, pardon!'

Desmond carefully removed the glass and bottle from her.

'It's only wine, your majesty,' said Laura. 'It's not even that shrong, er, strong.'

The king looked at the bottle of apple wine. There was a long pause. 'Is this what you call alcohol, a drink containing ethanol? Makes sense, they are not used to it.'

The king went over to one of the sleeping aliens. He felt around the creature's body and removed a small cylinder from somewhere in the creature's clothing. He did the same with the other two.

'These weapons are small but deadly,' he said. He inclined his large head towards the three sleepers 'You had better leave them to me. I will communicate with my ship.' He stood silently for a moment, then said. 'Please, let us sit.' There was a pause for a few minutes and then Aramantha took the time to tell her father about her adventures. He looked over at Mitzi and gave her a warm smile. Then there was a humming noise from overhead.

Ingrid realised what the noise must be. 'It's the spaceship,' she said with a gasp. 'Can you hear it?'

There came a second, higher pitched noise.

'That sounds like a squeaky wheel,' said Mitzi, as she put her hands over her ears. The noise rose to a crescendo, and the three enemy aliens disappeared.

'You have been very lucky,' said the king. 'That is the captain of their ship and two of his security team. They are fearsome people. Very dangerous. I have transferred them directly to our prison cell.'

'Now, Aramantha. It is time,' he said. In English.

Aramantha turned to Mitzi first, who was holding back tears.

'Do not cry, Mitzi. I go to my wedding.' She hugged her. She turned to Ingrid.

She said something to her father in their own language. Then she said, 'Farewell, my knight counsellor of Boldera. It may be that we will meet again, sooner than you think.' Then she stepped back and addressed everyone, 'You have been my asylum and shelter. I thank you.'

'I will miss you,' said Ingrid. 'Don't forget you are going to teach the court to have fun!' And she knelt down to embrace the princess in a hug. Her father looked shocked, but the princess happily hugged her back.

'It's all right, father. It's culturally appropriate!' said Aramantha with a laugh.

The high-pitched noise came again. Everyone waved as the two alien figures, father and daughter, faded away to nothing. It was all over. They all looked at each other and each of them could see the sadness in the others' faces. Mitzi left the room in tears and headed for her bedroom.

'Well, that's that,' said Laura, with a sniff. She wiped away a tear. 'She was a lovely little thing, wasn't she? I suppose we had better try and get shome shleep for what's left of the night.' She gave a hiccup, which made everybody laugh.

'Drunk in the line of duty!' said Desmond and everyone laughed again.

The next morning, Desmond and Laura surfaced wearily at about nine o'clock, two hours later than normal. Laura went upstairs, yawning, to rouse her family. She started with the boys. She went into their room.

'Come on, you two, you have no excuse! You weren't up late.' She threw back the curtains in their room. 'Aramantha's gone home. Her daddy came for her last night. Breakfast will be do-it-yourself.'

The boys were devastated that they didn't get a chance to see the spaceship.

The next call was at Ruby's room. She went in. Ruby was fast asleep. Laura smiled for a moment.

She looks sweet when she's asleep, thought Laura.

'Come on, sweetheart! Breakfast!' Ruby groaned.

Laura went on, into Ingrid's room. There was no sign of her eldest daughter. She was not in bed. She was not in the en-suite shower room, and her bed looked as if it hadn't been slept in. A frantic search followed. Everyone was roped in. Seven sleepy people roamed through the house calling her name. At last, they had to admit it. Ingrid had gone.

– CHAPTER FOURTEEN –

ABOARD THE SPACESHIP

Ingrid came to her senses in a large chamber of some kind. One moment she was brushing her hair and getting ready for bed, next moment she was here. She was still holding her hairbrush! She felt dizzy and sat down hard on the metallic floor. The chamber was lined with shiny metal. It was the size of a small bedroom. The glare was dazzling. When she felt able to focus her eyes, she saw Aramantha across the room, smiling.

'Welcome to the 'Boldera', the royal barge of my people.' Aramantha came over and helped Ingrid to her feet. She seemed different somehow.

She's more grown up, more... Ingrid searched for the right word. *More* regal, *that's it,* she thought.

It was true. Aramantha carried herself erect. There was a confidence, no it was more than that – an *arrogance* about her every movement.

'When we return to Boldera, you will be by my side, my knight counsellor, my lady in waiting, and my minister of fun! Isn't it wonderful!'

Ingrid was still groggy from the transfer to the ship. She didn't reply for a moment.

'How did I get here?' she asked weakly. 'I was in my bedroom...'

'His majesty, my father, acceded to my request to transport you here, using the atomic conveyor.'

'The...?'

'Atomic conveyor. I am a royal princess. I have no knowledge of its workings. That is for the workers.'

She uses the word 'workers' in the same way we would use 'vermin', thought Ingrid.

'My father is negotiating a safe passage back to Boldera with the enemy, using the soldiers you captured as a bargaining tool. Come, I will show you your quarters. They are next to mine.'

Ingrid followed her in a daze. They walked along corridors, until they came to a door. Aramantha waved her hand, the door slid open, and they went in. Inside the small room, it was as if they had walked into an advertisement for luxury bedrooms. There was a riot of colour everywhere. There was a bed covered in silken cushions in a range of vivid fabrics. Purples and pinks predominated, but there were soft chairs of bright yellow. Aramantha threw herself onto the bed.

'This is yours. I'm afraid it is rather small, there is not much space on a spaceship like this one. Do you like it? I can have the workers change it.'

Ingrid was so dazzled by all the bright colours and shiny surfaces that she wished she had brought her sunglasses!

'But, I...' she croaked.

'Ingrid Chan, we are not on Earth now. You must

get used to calling me "your highness" and when referring of me to others, you say 'Princess Aramantha', or 'the princess,' if the matter is urgent and it will save time.'

Ingrid cleared her throat. 'But, your royal highness, I can't come with you. I have to go back home. My family will miss me...'

'Your family have five other children; they will soon forget you.'

'That's not how it works on Earth, Ara... I mean, your highness. Besides, *I* will miss *them* badly.'

'But you will have me, and your duties. You will soon forget your old life on Earth,' said Aramantha gaily. 'Now that is the end of the matter. We will not discuss this again.' With that, she left. Ingrid flopped down into one of the marshmallow chairs, sinking in up to her hips. She gave way to tears, sobbing into her hands.

– CHAPTER FIFTEEN –

UNDER ATTACK!

Ingrid wiped her eyes on her sleeve. She went across to the bed and flung herself down on it. After a few minutes, she looked up as a noise sounded through the ship. It was a clanging noise. She wiped away her tears.

That doesn't sound good, she thought.

The door slid open and Aramantha rushed in, accompanied by two large Bolderan guards.

'Madame minister. The news is grave. The three captives have committed suicide, and the enemy ship is preparing to fight.'

'How did they commit suicide?' gasped Ingrid.

'They had slow-acting poison concealed inside their bodies. If they had got back to their ship in good time, they would have received the antidote which would have saved them.'

She looks really scared, thought Ingrid. 'Is their ship bigger than ours?' she asked.

'It's a mighty vessel of war. We're a lightly armed transport ship. We can try to run, but I fear that we are doomed.'

Ingrid stepped forward to give her a hug, but

Aramantha moved back and set her jaw. 'We will fight to the end. My father, the king, is very brave.'

'Take me to him!' said Ingrid, who was suddenly Colonel Ingrid of the Interplanetary Space Fleet.

Ingrid was taken to the spaceship's bridge, which was surprisingly small, no bigger than an average bathroom on Earth.

'Your majesty,' said Ingrid without preamble. 'Do you have explosives on board?'

The king was surprised at being addressed so directly by this Earth girl. He turned to his daughter. They conversed in Bolderanese for a moment.

The king turned to Ingrid.

'Yes, we do have explosives aboard,' he said. 'We have our low yield torpedoes, but they are not strong enough to penetrate the enemy's shields.'

'But if they went off inside the ship, they would do some damage, wouldn't they?'

'Yes, of course, but—'

'Then surrender.'

'Bolderans never surrender!'

'Surrender, your majesty,' insisted Colonel Ingrid. 'Then invite some of their people aboard. When they beam in, beam the explosives onto their ship.'

'That won't work,' said the king. They would detect the incoming items.'

Ingrid thought for a moment. 'All right. Say the princess has agreed to give herself over to them, if they will spare your crew.'

Aramantha cried, 'Never!'

'Your majesty, your highness, it's a trick, a ruse. Prepare some bombs from your torpedoes, then when they lower their shields to beam the princess over, beam torpedoes over to their ships at the same time.'

There was some rapid Bolderanese between father and daughter. Ingrid was still thinking. 'Do they know what the princess looks like?' she asked.

'No, I don't think they do,' he replied.

'How were they going to find her back on Earth?'

'They would be tracking her, via the metal in her implant. It does not exist on Earth. It would have been easy for them to find her.'

'Can you implant me?'

'No!' cried Aramantha. 'Your majesty, my father, do not let her do this. She wants to sacrifice herself for me.'

'I don't! I'm hoping you will pull me back before the bombs explode! You can put the bomb in my backpack.'

'We will need to line your bag with a metal foil to prevent them detecting the bomb. It will be very heavy.'

Colonel Ingrid, of the Interplanetary Space Patrol, set her jaw. 'I'll manage,' she said. So, it was agreed.

The king addressed the enemy ship. He delivered a long and flowery surrender speech. He scolded the enemy for their ruthless aggression. He told them of his love for his daughter. He spoke of their long lineage, but finally he announced their surrender. He gave Ingrid as much time as he could.

Ingrid was taken to the medical bay, where a

technician approached her with something that looked like a gun.

She held Ingrid's arm firmly while she pressed the device against the Earth girl's head. Ingrid was conscious of a sudden shock, as if someone had struck her a blow on the head. The technician let go.

'Is that it?' asked Ingrid. The technician did not understand English, she merely shrugged.

Aramantha came into the little medical bay and spoke to the technician. She turned to Ingrid.

'We've activated the implant. It will detect your thoughts and relay them to us. It is hard to get used to. Do not let it distract you.'

'Um, how big is it?' Aramantha held up two fingers close together to indicate something of the thickness of a pound coin.

'Wow, that's about the size of a computer chip,' she said. 'OK. Come on. We've got to get going.' They headed back into Ingrid's quarters.

The king's people had quickly removed the explosives from a torpedo, added a timing device and placed it carefully into Ingrid's rucksack, which had been lined with metal foil.

'You will not have much time, oh beloved counsellor,' said Aramantha. To Ingrid's surprise, she embraced her in a quick hug. 'Goodbye and please come back,' she said. Then she slipped away and made herself scarce.

Ingrid tried the weight of the bag. It was no worse than when Aramantha was inside it. She put it on and waited. After a few moments, there came a pleasant musical sound from the door. Someone was outside. She went to the door and waved her hand as she had seen Aramantha do. The door opened. Outside were two of the enemy soldiers, with their long faces and large eyes. They fell in either side of her and escorted her back to the chamber she had arrived in. The three of them were transferred, molecule by molecule, to the enemy ship. Ingrid was now, as her family had feared, firmly in the hands of the enemy.

– CHAPTER SIXTEEN –
TRAPPED!

Ingrid was taken to a bare room that was only a small step up from a prison cell. She carefully placed her rucksack against the wall. She tried to communicate with Aramantha through the implant. It took a lot of concentration, and it was a precious few minutes before she got through.

'At last! You must hurry!' was Aramantha's urgent thought when Ingrid finally managed to get through. 'Soon they will leave your solar system and take you with them. They are transferring their people now. You must get away from the bomb. It's almost ready to explode!'

Ingrid thought for a moment, then she banged on the door of her chamber. It was opened and one of the guards looked in.

How do I say toilet in their language? she thought. The computer answered her with remarkable speed, giving her the enemy alienese for waste disposal. She voiced the sounds, hoping she had copied the strange noises right. The guard understood and he led the way along the corridor. Soon he opened the door to a room with no windows and only one door. Ingrid followed him, like a princess, with head held high. She waved him aside and entered the room. The door closed.

'Their shields are going up. We can't get you out!' rang in her head from a frantic Aramantha. 'They are locking their weapons on us!'

Before Ingrid had time to digest this, there came a huge explosion, and klaxons went off all over the enemy ship. There was a huge lurch followed by a squirmy sensation in Ingrid's stomach, then the walls of the toilet chamber faded, and she lost consciousness.

When she came around, Ingrid was in the little medical bay of the royal yacht Bolderana.

She opened her eyes. She was lying on a low bed, and Aramantha was holding her hand.

'Oh, I am so glad, Counsellor Ingrid!' she cried, and against all royal protocol, she threw herself on Ingrid and hugged her firmly. She stood up and brushed herself down. 'Ahem, it was a difficult transfer. Your signal was not as clear as we would have liked. It was a happy thing you had the implant. It helped us pinpoint you. It was good that you moved away from the explosive. The explosion brought down their shields and we were able to get you out. We had to pull you out quickly because that part of their ship was depressurising. It took us some time to transfer you, so you have had to lie down for some time. I was beginning to think you were not going to open your eyes.'

Ingrid was still a bit groggy from the 'difficult

transfer' back to the royal yacht. She took a moment to gather her thoughts.

'Er, speaking of getting me out, your highness. I really would like to go back to my family now.'

Unseen by Aramantha or Ingrid, the king had come in. He spoke to the princess. She hung her head and replied in contrite Bolderanese.

His majesty spoke to Ingrid. 'I was led to believe that your presence here was voluntary,' he said. 'If it is your wish to return, then of course you must return to your home.' He spoke sternly to Aramantha, who bit her lip and hung her head.

Aramantha turned to Ingrid. 'I am sorry, Ingrid Chan. My honourable father is right. He reminds me of what we have all been through, simply because someone tried to kidnap me. You have saved me, and I must not kidnap you and keep you from your family.'

'How far can the implants reach?' asked Ingrid.

'If we boost the signal, I can reach you from orbit around your planet.'

'Then you must come and say hello sometimes. Oh, and introduce me to your fiancé!'

The two girls embraced. Ingrid completed the short trip back to Yorkshire on the bridge of the ship. As she stood in the transfer chamber, tears flowed down her face. She waved to Aramantha, as the chamber faded away like a television picture, and she rematerialized in her own bedroom. She staggered a little, but she was a seasoned traveller now and she quickly regained her balance. She ran to the bedroom door and shouted, 'I'm home!'

There were screams and shouts from all over the house. Ingrid looked in the mirror. She thrust out her jaw and folded her arms. Colonel Ingrid of the Interplanetary Space Patrol had returned to space dock!

– CHAPTER ONE –
FIRE IN THE HILLS

The end of August approached, and Ingrid became nervous about her new school. She was scheduled to visit the school in early September with all the other new girls.

As a result, Ruby was becoming almost impossible as her promotion to big sister loomed closer.

Mitzi played with her dolls, and was reading by herself more.

Dilly was really enjoying her chemistry set, and Mum helped her to understand the science behind the experiments. She also managed to create some quite exciting effects including an explosion, which the children enjoyed, especially the twins!

The twins were the same as always. Full of the joys of life, doing their schoolwork, and enjoying their free time when it came. Despite their harum-scarum ways, underneath it all, they cared for their sisters. One night they surprised Ingrid with a lovely gesture. They invited her to a midnight feast in their bedroom. It was just like *Malory Towers* where midnight feasts were the done thing. So, when everyone was asleep, and even Mum and Dad had retired to bed, the three of them met up in the little bedroom.

The twins had set out a cloth on the floor, with plates borrowed from the kitchen cupboard. There were sandwiches, crisps, and cakes too, all filched from the kitchen, along with a big bottle of fizzy pop. The bedroom light was switched off, and they lit the room with torches.

'Oh, you two! How lovely,' said Ingrid. 'It's just like Darrell Rivers and her friends.' The twins wriggled with pleasure. They ate and played card games. They all enjoyed it, and it was even more special because it was just the three of them and it was a secret.

I don't spend enough time with the twins, thought Ingrid. She was touched by their gesture, and in spite of being nervous about what was going to happen in September, she joined in their silly games and ate the rather stale food (which the twins had been hoarding all day) and drank the fizzy pop.

At last they called it a night, and Ingrid smiled at them. She said thank you, gave them both a hug, and went straight to bed.

It was one o'clock in the morning. The boys looked at each other. The party was over, but they still felt full of energy. They climbed onto Jacky's bed to look out of the window at the stars.

'D'you think there's any more spaceships up there?' queried Jacky.

'Bound to be!' replied Oscar. Then he exclaimed

'Look!' and pointed.

Out in the dales, was a flickering light.

'Oscar,' asked Jacky. 'Are you ready to go to sleep?'

'No, not really.'

'Good, I think the fire is just over the ridge, look.'

They both stared at the flickering light in the night, estimating the distance.

'It's not far,' agreed Oscar.

With that, the plan was made; the twins did not need many words. They pulled on some trousers and jumpers over their pyjamas and slipped out of the house through the kitchen door. They climbed the ridge. It was about half a kilometre away and from the top they could see the fire quite clearly. It looked like a campfire. They could not see anybody, so they crept on down the hill to get a better look.

The fire was neatly contained in a little trench dug out of the turf. Above the fire, on a contraption made of sticks, was an animal, skinned and cooking in the heat.

'Rabbit,' said Jacky.

Oscar nodded.

With an almighty yell, a heavy stick flew past Jacky's ear, and a figure leapt on them from the darkness. Oscar was thrown to the ground by the ferocity of the attack. The two rolled and wrestled on the grass. Jacky picked his moment and grabbed the attacker and peeled them away from his brother. The attacker fought back like a demon, and both boys got their bruises. In the end, the two boys managed to push the aggressor over and held them down.

'Slepptu mer!' cried their prisoner.

Without understanding a word, the boys did indeed let go. They stood up in surprise.

'It's a girl!' They cried in unison.

'Bjófar! Farðu burt! Það er kanínan mín!' yelled the girl.

She picked up her stick from the fire and brandished it in their direction. In the firelight the twins could see her clearly. She wore a long shirt over trousers, with a sort of woollen tunic over the top. She had a leather bag on a strap across her shoulder. Her blonde hair was cut to shoulder length. Her eyes blazed with anger. She was a little older than they were – ten or eleven perhaps.

The twins got it. She was defending her camp and her food. They looked at each other and grinned. Oscar put out his hand. 'Awesome fight!' he said.

The girl stared fiercely for a moment, then she grinned, shrugged, put out her hand, and grasped his arm. He did the same. She pointed to his face and grinned.

'Þér blæðir,' she said.

'She means "your nose is bleeding",' explained Jacky with a laugh. Soon they were all laughing. Jacky got a tissue from his pocket and dabbed his nose. He pointed to the girl's eye.

'Black eye,' he said. The girl patted her eye ruefully, shrugged and sat down. She pointed to the roasting rabbit.

'Endilega deilið matnum mínum,' she said. The boys didn't understand her words, but they understood her gesture. 'Have some of my food.'

The boys had just stuffed themselves with the midnight feast, so Jacky shook his head and patted his stomach. 'No thanks,' he said.

The girl shrugged and removed the well-cooked rabbit from the fire. She reached into her bag and produced a knife, which looked like one of the chef's knives from their own kitchen. She cut off some meat and shoved it into her mouth.

'Ég fann það' she said proudly, speaking with her mouth full. She showed the boys the knife as if it was a trophy.

Oscar took the knife and examined it. It had quite a thick blade and was very sharp. He ran his thumb along the blade as he had seen happen in *Lord of the Rings*, one of his favourite films. He immediately regretted it. He cut his thumb, making it bleed freely. This made the girl laugh like a drain. She indicated he should suck the wound. Then she reached into her bag and produced a root of some kind and some leaves. She chewed the root for a moment and spat it onto her hand.

'Réttu mér hönd þína,' she said gently, and she held out her hand for him to give her his. She used her other hand to rub the chewed-up root onto his thumb.

It stung. Oscar winced and tried to pull his hand away, but the girl held it firmly. She laughed at his weakness and called him a baby. *'Þú ert eins og barn!'*

Then she pressed the leaves onto the cut and indicated he should press his fingers firmly on it.

Jacky was amazed by this procedure. He put his hand out for the root, and the girl gave him some. He sniffed it, then he put a tiny bit in his mouth. The girl saw him. She cried out, '*Nei! Hættu*!' She made spitting motions and encouraged him to copy. He spat out the root.

'Yuck!' he said. 'That was horrible, it burns!' He pulled a face, which made the girl laugh again.

Oscar looked around. The dales were lit by a starlight glow. He could see for miles. There was no one else to be seen.

'Where are your mother and father?' he asked.

'*Móður mína og föður*?

He wanted to be sure she had understood, 'Yes, mum, dad, you know.' And he pretended to be his dad, then his mum, walking up and down with a stern face, pretending to tell Jacky off.

The girl smiled at his antics, then her face fell as she said, '*Móður mína og föður...*' and then she shrugged in a gesture that was clear in any language.

'You don't know where they are?' asked Jacky in surprise.

'You'd better come with us,' said Oscar. 'My mum will know what to do.' He gestured to the girl. 'Come, come,' he said.

'*Kem ég*?' she said.

'Yes, er *kem, kem*,' said Oscar.

'*Bíða*,' said the girl, putting up her hand in a 'wait' gesture. First, working by firelight, she cut up the rabbit meat, and wrapped it in leaves, then she took up a tin can full of water and threw the contents on the fire to douse it. She dried the inside of the can carefully using her sleeve, then she placed the uneaten meat into the can, and put them both into her bag.

'Hjálpaðu mér.' She pulled Jacky over to where she had cut out the turf for the fire and made him help her. The turf lay in two long strips. Together they carried it back to the fireplace and replaced it. She was incredibly neat with it, and the same with the next one. When she had finished, you would have never known that anyone had been there! The girl picked up her stick, which had been sharpened to a point at one end. It was a spear!

'That just missed me,' said Jacky with a gasp, pointing to the spear, then himself. The girl laughed and slapped him on the back. She put her arms around both their shoulders.

'V*ini!'* she exclaimed.

'Pleased to meet you, Vinny. I'm Jacky, this is Oscar.' Jacky pointed to his brother then himself.

She pointed to herself. 'Aifa,' she said.

Confused, Oscar turned to Jacky. 'She said her name was Vinny!'

'*Vini*?' he asked the girl.

She took his arm, then Oscar's. She pointed to the three of them in turn. 'Ja, vini Oscar, Yacky, Aifa, vini!' And she put her arms around their shoulders. 'kem, kem!'

'I think it means mates,' said Oscar.

'Vini, ja vini!' She smiled.

'Ja, ja!' said Jacky.

They led her back to the farmhouse. From the top of the ridge you could see the farmhouse below.

Aifa threw herself to the floor. *'Húsið þitt?'* she inquired. She pointed to the old farmhouse, then to each of them in turn.

'Er, *ja,*' said Oscar, who pointed to the house, then to himself and Jacky. 'It's our house.' Aifa shook her head and began to crawl backwards, down the ridge and away.

'Aifa! Wait!' called Jacky. But she was gone, like a ghost in the night.

'Oh, why did she do that? I liked her. She was fun!' said Oscar. Jacky grinned.

'Oscar's got a girlfriend, Oscar's in lurve!' he crowed.

'Shut up!' said Oscar, taking a swing at him. In a moment they were wrestling around on the grass. Their fights never amounted to much and, within minutes, the two boys had made up. They climbed back up the crumbly old wall to their bedroom window and, in no time, they were fast asleep in their beds.

– CHAPTER TWO –

WHERE'S MY KNIFE?

The next morning, after their twilight activities, the twins overslept and, in consequence, missed an important task. They realised this too late when Mum came into their bedroom looking for her missing plates!

'There they are!' she exclaimed from the door of the room. The twins opened their eyes sleepily.

'What?' said Jacky.

'All my tea plates!'

'Oh, erm... Yeah, sorry, Mum. We, erm, had an indoor picnic,' admitted Oscar.

'A late indoor picnic? Perhaps at midnight? It's all right. Ingrid told me all about it. No wonder you're late up this morning! I think it was sweet of you to do that for Ingrid, but you now need to wash those plates, and not in the dishwasher!'

Oscar groaned and pulled the covers over his head. 'Come on. Out of bed. It's a beautiful day. Up, up, up'. She threw open the curtains. 'Oh, by the way, where is my best kitchen knife? Did you use it for your picnic?'

Oscar pushed the covers off his face and sat up.

'Your kitchen knife?' he parroted.

'Yes, Mr Echo! My. Kitchen. Knife.' She punctuated her words by tickling him. 'I don't see it here. What have you done with it?'

'Erm, we haven't had it, Mum. Honest,' said Jacky.

'Oh, well, it didn't walk off on its own!'

'Truthfully, Mum, we haven't taken it,' said Oscar.

'Well, get your bedroom tidied, bring down the plates and wash them. No breakfast until it's done.'

'Oh, Mum!' cried the boys in unison.

'That will teach you to have secret midnight feasts, without me!' And she picked up a pillow and tossed it at Jacky as she left. 'And maybe when you've finished tidying up, you'll find that knife. It's my best one.'

The boys got up and wearily began to collect the plates and other detritus together.

'Let me help,' said a voice from the doorway. It was Ingrid. 'I'm sorry guys, but Mum asked me straight out where the plates were, and I had to tell her. It'll take two minutes if we do it together.'

Three minutes later the bedroom was tidy, the beds were made and the three of them were in the kitchen washing the plates. Ingrid washed and the boys dried.

'Mum says one of her knives is missing,' remarked Ingrid.

'It wasn't us!' exclaimed the twins together, rather more loudly than was necessary.

'OK, OK. I believe you, thousands wouldn't.'

'Honest, Inga, we haven't got it.'

Head teacher Ingrid looked down at them.

'Haven't seen it, or haven't got it?' she asked. The

boys squirmed. 'We haven't got it, and we don't know where it is,' pouted Oscar. Which was true enough. Even if what the boys suspected was true, they couldn't say exactly where the knife was at that moment!

'OK, but it's a mystery. Where can it have gone?'

After breakfast, the twins ran out onto the dales. They dashed over the ridge and chased each other down the steep hill on the other side. Eventually they arrived at the place where they had meet Aifa the night before. They searched and they called her name, but there was no sign of her.

'She didn't want to come back to the house because that's where she stole the knife,' said Jacky. Oscar looked at him and nodded. They shrugged and turned back towards the house.

The girls came out and met them, and someone suggested a game of French cricket.

Two more days passed. It wasn't long now until Ingrid was due to go away to school, and they all seemed determined to have some good games as a family, before they were split up. It was a happy time. No one got cross – or not very much – and if they did it was soon made up.

It was the third night after the midnight feast. Jacky and Oscar were asleep. Then a rattling sound woke Jacky up. He looked across at Oscar, who was still asleep.

'Hey, Oscar, you awake?' he whispered. No reply.

He said it louder, which, of course woke Oscar up.

'What's up?' groaned Oscar.

'Did you hear that noise?'

'What noise?'

There came another rattle right on cue. It sounded like pebbles against the window.

'That noise!'

'Oh.' Oscar climbed out of bed and joined Jacky by the window. Together they looked out. In the dim light they could just make out a figure in the dark.

'Is that…'

'Yes, it's whatshername… Aifa.' Jacky opened the window.

He called down to her. 'Hi, Aifa.'

'Hjálpaðu mér,' said Aifa in a sad little voice, dropping a handful of pebbles.

They saw she was standing on one leg, supporting herself by her spear, and lifting the other foot off the ground.

The boys looked at each other.

'Get Mum!' said Jacky.

'I'll get Aifa, you get mum. I'll let Aifa into the kitchen,' commanded Oscar, the older brother by fifteen minutes.

He went down to the back door and beckoned to Aifa. She hung back at first, but he assured her it was all right.

Aifa limped into the kitchen, leaning on her improvised crutch. Oscar switched on the light and gave Aifa a start.

'It's all right. It's just the light,' he said. He helped her into a seat at the kitchen table.

Just then Jacky and Mum appeared. Aifa growled and picked up her spear. Oscar put his hand on her arm. 'It's all right, it's our mum,' he soothed.

'Móðir þín?' she asked.

'Yes, mum,' he said. She subsided into her seat.

Oscar could see her now the light was on. Her eye, from the fight three days before, was a glorious purple! Her clothes were tattered, torn, and covered in blood, and through the holes he could see she was bruised black and blue all down the right-hand side. She looked like she had been in a fight with an army!

– CHAPTER THREE –

THE ROARING DEMON

Jacky pointed to Aifa's bruised face and body. 'What happened?' he asked.

She shook her head. *'Það var djöfull'* she said. She became animated as she demonstrated what had happened, complete with sound effects. She showed them how the *'djöfull'* had rushed at her with bright glowing eyes and she imitated the sound of its roaring, and when it came close it screeched. She mimed to them how she threw her spear at it, but it didn't stop, and then it hit her.

'það fékk mér hræðilegt högg.'

'Why, it's Icelandic, or a form of it anyway,' said Mum. She says she was attacked by a demon with bright eyes and a roaring voice!' She turned to Aifa. *'Hvað heitir þú?'* she asked. Aifa's eyes grew big and round in astonishment.

'Aifa, Aifa Hartvigsen, Frú…'

'Ég heiti Laura, Laura Chan. *Hann heitir* Oscar, *hann heitir* Jacky. *Þú ert meiddur,'* she said. That was all too clear! All of them could see that Aifa had been badly hurt in her brush with the 'demon'.

'There aren't any demons, are there?' asked Jacky.

'No, silly. Bright lights, rushing noise. It was a car! She doesn't understand about cars,' said Oscar scornfully.

'They have cars in Iceland, don't they?' said Jacky to his mum.

'Of course they do. I don't understand what's happening here, but right now we need to fix her up. She may need to go to hospital.'

Mum sent the boys out, then she undressed Aifa, and attended to her wounds.

The boys hung about in the hallway shivering. Oscar and Jacky both looked down at their pyjamas. 'Jumpers,' they both said together and ran off to get them.

When Mum called them back in, they were warmly dressed. Aifa was also dressed in some of Ingrid's old jeans and a long-sleeved t-shirt. She was bandaged up almost from head to toe.

'I don't think anything is broken. I've been chatting to Aifa and, from what I can understand, she was able to jump just as the car hit her. She's badly bruised, and she twisted her ankle when she landed, but that's all. She says she drove it away with her spear! Apparently the car didn't stop, which is disgraceful. I'd like to give that driver a piece of my mind. They might have killed her! I've plastered her cuts and bandaged her ankle. She is adamant she doesn't want to go to hospital. I'm not sure she should anyway with COVID. Boys, can you please tell me what happened?' she asked. So they did.

'She's really cool, Mum. She can catch rabbits and

cook them. And she can really fight!' said Oscar.

Jacky grinned. 'Oscar's in love with her, Mum. Oscar has a girlfriend!' he crowed. Mum stopped the fight that would have followed, by raising her hand.

'Sit still!' she ordered. They did as they were told.

'Hvernig komstu hingað?' Mum asked Aifa. 'I asked how she got here,' she explained to the boys.

Aifa released a torrent of ancient Icelandic, and she stood up to mime it all out, complete with gestures, then she winced at the pain it caused.

The boys looked at Mum waiting for her to translate, but she just sat and stared at their guest, unable to speak for a moment.

Time passed.

Mum gulped, then she croaked, 'Aifa says she stowed away in a ship. They came up the river from the coast, and when...' She turned to Aifa. *'þegar stríðsmennirnir fóru í land?'* Aifa nodded, glumly. Mum continued, 'When the warriors came ashore, she waited for a moment and sneaked out, avoiding the two sentries who were watching the boat. She says they didn't see her because they were busy playing dice. She followed the band of warriors as long as she could, but she lost them in the grasslands and hills. She felt very tired, she hid in some rocks. She lay down to sleep, and when she woke, she went back to the river, thinking to stowaway on the ship again, but there was no sign of the boats or the warriors, not an arrowpoint not a spearhead, nothing. Since then, she has been living off the land. Snaring rabbits and killing them with a knife she stole from a house!'

She looked at Aifa and spoke to her, '*Sýndu mér hnífinn*!' she said. Aifa looked shamefaced, then reached into her bag and took out the knife, which she very reluctantly handed over to Mum.

'My best knife!' exclaimed Mum. The twins giggled. 'I expect she's blunted it.'

'No, Mum, she hasn't. It's really, really sharp!' said Oscar.

Mum gingerly touched the edge. Aifa reached for the knife. After a moment's hesitation, Mum handed it over.

'*Ég skerpa það á steinum,*' Aifa said, miming sharpening the knife with a stone. She made to give it back.

'*Halda því,*' said Mum. Aifa's eyes grew round, and she hugged the knife to her as if it were a rare treasure, which in her world it was.

'I told her to keep it,' said Mum. 'Well, as I understand it, they came up the river Ouse from the Humber estuary, then the river Aire, as far as Coniston Cold. It's weird, you can't do that journey like that any more. The Aire flows underground part of the way, I think.' She turned to Oscar. 'I've had an idea. Do you remember the *Ladybird Book of Vikings*?'

'Yeah, Mum. It's a really old book.'

'It's no older than I am!'

'Exactly,' said Jacky with a grin.

'Cheeky! Do you know where it is?

'I think it's in the quiet room.'

'Can you please get it?'

Oscar was off like a shot. He returned two minutes later with the old book, well-thumbed by two generations of children. Mum showed it to Aifa, who pounced on it with a cry of joy. She thumbed through the colourful pictures. She pointed to a picture of the Viking longship on page five.

'*Það er báturinn minn*!' she cried.

'She says that's her boat.'

Aifa showed them another picture of a Viking warrior, complete with shield and weapons:

'*Það er faðir minn!*' she exclaimed proudly. She examined the picture more closely, a tear escaped from her eye. She brushed it away angrily. '*Hann líkist föður mínum,*' she whispered.

'That one looks like her father,' she explained to the twins. 'I don't know how this could possibly have happened, but when she fell asleep, she slept for more than a thousand years!'

– CHAPTER FOUR –

AIFA MEETS THE CHANS

The next day the family came down to breakfast as usual. The girls, who had slept through all the excitement, came into the kitchen to find Mum and Dad cooking breakfast – and a stranger at the table.

'Girls, I would like you to meet Aifa Hartvigsen. She's from Scandinavia. She doesn't speak English. She's been in a road accident. We are looking after her for the time being.'

'Hi, Aifa,' said Ingrid. 'My name's Ingrid, Inga for short.'

'Inga? *Vinur minn heitir Inge!'* exclaimed Aifa.

'Her friend is called Inge,' explained Mum.

'What language is that?' asked Ruby.

'It's a form of Icelandic.'

Ruby turned to Aifa. 'You. Come. From. Ice... land? Yes?'

'Ruby!' scolded Ingrid. 'It doesn't help if you speak louder and slower. It's still English! She won't understand you.'

'All right, Ingrid! Mum, how do I say, "you're from Iceland"?'

'Er, it's not as simple as that, dear! For one thing, Aifa calls Iceland, Snaeland. But if you want to ask her you say, '*Kemur þú frá Snaeland*?'

'Sounds Scottish,' said Ruby. She turned to Aifa. '*Kemmer thoo frae Snaeland*?'

This made Aifa laugh. Mum smiled to see it.

Mum translated for Aifa, who had spoken in scornful tones, 'No one lives in 'Snaeland'. It is barren, a wasteland.'

'But…'

'Girls, I don't understand how it's happened, but it seems that Aifa is from a different time. I'm guessing she was born in around 850.'

The girls gasped. '850?' repeated Ruby. 'That's like hundreds of years ago!'

'One thousand one hundred and seventy years ago,' computed Ingrid.

Just then the boys came sleepily into the room.

'Help yourselves to breakfast, boys, 'said Mum. The boys did as they were told and sat down at the table. Oscar sat next to Aifa and gave her a smile. She smiled back at him.

'One thousand one hundred and seventy years ago? Wow!' exclaimed Dilly. 'How did she get here?'

'We know there are "wormholes" in space,' said Dad. 'Short cuts you can take to cover vast distances, many parsecs, in an instant. Some people think that there are wormholes in time as well. Like a doorway to a different time. I think Aifa must have found one of those.'

'The raid that she was a part of might even have been at, or around, the time that York was captured by the Vikings. Iceland wasn't settled until after her time.' Mum turned to their guest. *'Aifa, heyrðirðu nafnið Jorvik?'*

Aifa thought about the question, then said, *'Já, já, ég heyrði Jorvik!'*

'She says she heard them talking about York. So that must be around 865. So, she was born in around 855.' Mum turned to Aifa. *'Hvað ertu gamall'* she asked.

'Ég er tíu ára.'

'I thought so. She's ten, like you, Ruby.' The twins tried to get their heads around this. Aifa was the same age as Ruby?

'If she were a modern girl, she would be talking about the silly things that Ruby likes to talk about clothes and celebrity gossip. Those silly reality programmes she likes to watch – and, yuck, kittens on social media sites! I can't imagine Aifa and her Viking friends doing any of that!' said Oscar, turning to Aifa.

'Do you talk to the other girls about clothes and things?' he asked.

'Óskar vildi vita hvað þú talar um við hinar stelpurnar!' Mum said with a smile.

Aifa made a long and animated reply.

'She says the other girls are only interested in the warrior that's the best-looking or has the biggest muscles… or in showing off the new clothes they made from cloth that their fathers have brought back from a raid… or about their pet cats!' She stifled a laugh, but she couldn't resist a glance at her second daughter, who put her head down and concentrated on eating, but she blushed as red as her name.

Oscar seemed stunned by how little had changed in more than a thousand years! Then Aifa spoke again, this time with dramatic gestures and sound effects.

'She doesn't understand them,' interpreted Mum. 'She wants to fight with the warriors when she grows up. To be a shield maiden like, I think it was *Lagertha*. Aifa says her father is a great warrior. He is the shield Thane to the chief, that's like the chief's right-hand man.'

It cheered Oscar up that Aifa was not what he called silly-girly, and he moved his chair even closer to her.

Aifa was deep in her own thoughts and didn't seem to notice. *'Hvar er faðir minn?'* she said sadly.

Mum looked at Dad. 'She wants to know where her father is. What can I tell her?'

Dad shook his head, then said, 'You must tell her the truth. And promise that we will try to get her back to where she comes from.'

Mum knelt down beside Aifa and took her hand. She spoke to her for some time in Icelandic.

Later in the evening, she told her husband about the conversation.

'I told her that much time has passed and the raid on York was a great success. For the Vikings at any rate! I told her that the Vikings settled here and became farmers and then city dwellers. She thought that was very funny! She told me that she couldn't see her father as a farmer! I told her that she was asleep for more than a thousand years. I said my father, being Swedish, was a descendant of the Vikings. Oh, and I said the "demon" was a device, a chariot without horses, driven by a careless human, not some immortal creature! That was enough for her to think about. Oh, Des, what's to become of her?'

– CHAPTER FIVE –

PREPARING FOR A LONG TREK

The children all went outside. The boys wanted to romp and wrestle, but Aifa was still in pain and could not join in, much as she wanted to. Instead she showed them how to throw a spear, and how to catch rabbits. On one of her raids on the local farms, she had taken some tarred string, which she used to snare the rabbits, before killing them and eating them. She showed them the string and demonstrated how to make the rabbit trap.

The girls were horrified.

'That's just gross!' exclaimed Ruby. 'It's cruel!' Aifa laughed at the expressions on their faces.

'Come on,' said Ingrid. 'It's time for a plan.'

Captain Ingrid sat them all down in front of her, Aifa included, then addressed her troop, walking up and down with her hands behind her back. 'I think we need to look for the time tunnel, or whatever it is, that brought Aifa here and send her back.' She looked at Aifa. 'We will find your father,' she said confidently.

'Faðir minn?'

'Er, *ja.* Father. Your father. First, we need to eat.

Lieutenant Ruby, Sergeant Dilly, organise enough provisions for two days please.' The two girls rushed off to cajole their mother into letting them have a picnic.

'Why can't Aifa stay with us?' complained Corporal Oscar, and he put his arm around her.

'Oscar loves Aifa!' hooted Jacky, and he fell backwards laughing.

'Order in the ranks!' snapped Ingrid. 'Now, Aifa, which way did you come here?'

She took out her phone and showed Aifa a map of northern Britain. This meant nothing to Aifa though. She had no idea what she was looking at, although she was fascinated by the phone itself, and kept looking at the back to see where the magic was!

Oscar had an inspiration.

'Aifa,' he said.

She turned to him. *'Ja, Oskar?'*

He pointed to her. 'You. Came here...' he pointed to the ground. 'You walked...' He mimed walking and getting very tired. Then he gestured to the countryside and shrugged his shoulders. 'Where from?'

'Oh. Ja. Ég skil. Erm...' Aifa found a stick.

Mitzi had been listening hard all morning to everything that Aifa said.

'Egg skill. That means I understand,' she said quietly – but nobody noticed.

Aifa took her trusty spear and drew in the soil. She drew a blade shape, then wavy lines, then a line down. She drew a boat shape on the wavy lines and put a sail on it. She puffed her cheeks and blew the boat.

'Eg er Njord!' she said with a laugh.

The Chans all looked at each other in puzzlement. Except Mitzi, who said, 'Egg, er, means I am,' she said. The boys were scornful, but Ingrid listened.

'Go on, Corporal Mitzi,' Ingrid urged.

'That's it. *Egg er* means I am, and I think *Nyord* must be somebody's name.'

Ingrid thought it sounded like *fjord,* and she tried typing in *'Njord'* on her phone. Bullseye!

'*Njord* is the Viking god of the wind!' she said with a laugh. 'She's pretending to be the wind!' They all laughed and blew at the boat drawing.

'Ja, ja!' said Aifa excitedly. She then traced the route from the spear shape.

'I think that's the top of Denmark,' said Ingrid. 'It's shaped like that.' She showed the others the map on her phone.

Aifa traced a line across the sea with the stick. She arrived at the straight line and stopped. Then she rubbed everything out and started again. She drew a river mouth, indicating that the estuary was an exceptionally large one. She traced the boat's journey along the river, following the tributaries. She mimed lots of weary rowing, then heaving the boat up onto the riverbank. Then she collapsed with pretend exhaustion. She slept, then she sprang up, pointed to the east and said, *'Sol, þar.'* She indicated the sun rising, yawned, stretched and picked up her spear, and an imaginary shield. Aifa used as deep a voice as she could, *'Þór á ferð þrumuskellur og hrun,'* she sang, and marched round with big steps. The boys loved it. They joined in. Soon they were all marching and singing, *'Þór á ferð þrumuskellur og hrun.'*

Just then, Ruby and Dilly came back, struggling under the weight of seven rucksacks filled with food and drinks.

'I told Mum that we wanted to show Aifa the local area, and that we might be gone all day. She said to keep in touch by phone.' She panted. Then she made a dramatic collapse. 'I'm exhausted carrying all these!' she grumbled.

'Thank you, both. Well done,' said Ingrid, then to Ruby, she added, sweetly, 'Perhaps if you're tired, Lieutenant, you'd rather stay at home while we go with Aifa.'

That did it. Ruby sprang up again, ready to go. She was not going to be left behind!

'All right, sit down everyone!' barked captain Ingrid. They immediately dropped to the ground.

Ingrid pointed to Aifa's drawing. 'I think that's the river Humber,' she explained. 'I've been looking at the map on my phone. I think they must have come up the Ouse, then the river Aire as far as Coniston Cold. That's not too far from here. It's only three miles away. If we take rests, we can do it in an hour and a half. Lieutenant, synchronise watches. It's... exactly... nine o'clock... now!'

They set off across the empty Dales, even emptier than usual thanks to the lockdown. Aifa was guiding them. They made good time at first. They stopped every twenty minutes for a five-minute rest. After an hour's walk, they stopped for twenty minutes to have something to eat. Ingrid was concerned about Mitzi, who had never walked this far in her life.

When they started again, Ingrid walked alongside Mitzi. 'Not too far now, Mitz. How are you doing?' she asked.

'I'm all right, Inge,' panted Mitzi stoutly. 'Long as we don't go too fast.'

They were now making slower progress. Aifa was unsure of the way. She ran up to a ridge and looked around helplessly. Then a cockerel crowed from a distant farm. Aifa laughed and pointed. *'Það er þannig!'* she said and ran down the vale towards the sound. In the distance they could all see a farm. Aifa slowed down to a careful walk. *'Ég stal kjúklingi hérna! Og ég drap það'* She did a very effective mime of stalking a chicken and killing it, then she was the chicken. She gave a last cluck and a squawk, before dropping dead on the ground. Ruby turned away, looking green. It had been a very realistic mime!

'So, you took a chicken from here?' asked Ingrid. 'Hmm.' She took out her phone. The river is that way, and York is that way. 'May I?' she asked, taking hold of Aifa's spear. Aifa reluctantly handed it over. Ingrid drew in the dirt. She pointed to the farm and drew a square on the floor to represent the building, with a line for the direction of the path leading to it. Then she drew a wavy line for the river. She added a boat by the side of the river. She looked at Aifa and mimed long by putting her arms out wide, then short by moving her hands close together.

Aifa nodded and copied the short gesture. She pointed to a ridge just above the house, mimed going over with her hand, then pointed to the river drawn in the earth.

She took back her spear and drew an outcrop of rock near the river and mimed falling asleep.

'The river's just over that ridge. She fell asleep by some rocks and when she woke up everything had changed,' Ingrid told the others. 'I think we need to head for those rocks.'

– CHAPTER SIX –

LOST IN TIME

Aifa took them to the top of the ridge to look at the countryside spread out below. There was a river like a broad silver thread, running its serpentine way through the green countryside under a brilliant blue cloudless sky.

'*Enginn bátur*!' Aifa said with tears in her eyes.

'She means "there's no boat",' said Mitzi. 'I remember that word from when she was talking about boats before.' Oscar put his arm around Aifa to console her.

'It's all right, Aifa,' said Ingrid kindly. 'We're not finished yet!' She pointed to the outcrop of rocks halfway down the hill. 'We need to go there.'

They carefully made their way down the hill. No one was in sight as they reached the stony outcrop.

Aifa advanced ahead and they followed her. She looked around, puzzled for a moment, then she pushed her way into a crack in the rocks.

'*Koma. Eltu mig,*' she said, calling for them to follow.

'She wants us to go with her. "*Koma*" means "come",' said Mitzi, who by now was the acknowledged expert on ancient Icelandic!

They pushed through the crack in the rocks and emerged in a small space, with rocks all round them and the sky above.

'Where did those clouds come from?' said Dilly.

'I feel funny,' said Jacky.

'Too much cheese and onion!' Ruby said sarcastically, before adding, 'Erm, actually, I don't feel so good either.'

'Það gerist aftur,' murmured Aifa, before she collapsed onto the hard ground.

One by one the Chans collapsed next to her.

When they awoke, it was dark.

'My head hurts!' exclaimed Mitzi.

'Mine too, Mitz,' moaned Dilly.

One by one they all came round. Ingrid groaned, then asked, 'Is everyone OK?'

Everyone nodded. She got to her feet.

Aifa sniffed the air. *'Viðareldar!'* she said.

They could all smell it now. A strong smell of wood smoke.

They stood up.

'Sergeant,' said Captain Ingrid. 'Recce, you know what to do.'

They had played this game many times during lockdown. Observing the enemy without being seen. The most athletic of the troop, Sergeant Dilly, scrambled to the top of the little group of rocks and peered out. She dropped back down again.

She looked at Ingrid with wide eyes. 'We're

surrounded, Captain!' she said. 'People all around us, sitting around fires. I think they're Vikings!'

'*Vikingar*?' said Aifa with a gasp. Before they could stop her, she scrambled up the rocks to get a look.

Dilly climbed up beside her. Aifa leaned precariously over the rock, looking this way and that, craning her neck. There were groups of men sitting round campfires. They wore baggy trousers and animal skin tops. They were eating, drinking and talking. There was a delicious smell of roasting meat. Occasionally great shouts of laughter would break out. Aifa focused on one group in particular.

'*Faðir minn*!' she said and pointed. By now all the Chans were lying high up on the rock looking down at the Vikings below.

Before anyone had the chance to think, or try and stop her, Aifa leapt to her feet. '*Faðir!*' she yelled at the top of her voice.

The men turned, many of them reached for their weapons. The rock was quickly surrounded by a bristling forest of razor-sharp spears.

One of the men pointed up. 'Aifa!' he said. '*Þetta er dóttir mín!*'

'The man just said "that's his daughter",' said linguist Mitzi helpfully.

'Her father!' exclaimed Ingrid. 'We must have slipped back in time. Dad was right!' She took out her phone. It was useless in the ninth century. She turned it off to save the battery.

Aifa slid down the rock, oblivious to the scrapes she

was getting on her legs and bottom. She ran to her father, and was swept up in an embrace. He had left his daughter safely at home, and now here she was, days later, and hundreds of miles away from where she should be!

The others came down. They were promptly seized and each one was held captive by a large, strong Viking warrior.

Aifa was talking to her father nineteen to the dozen.

'I think she said she was on the boat,' said Mitzi.

Aifa's father was having trouble understanding what had happened. They saw him shake his head. Then he hugged his daughter again.

The warriors stepped aside to make way for someone. He was tall and strong, and older than the others. The other men bowed their heads as he came past.

'I think that's the chief,' whispered Ingrid to the others.

The chief came over and looked at each Chan in turn. He squatted down to examine them all closely.

'*Þessir fiskar eru of litlir, henda þeim aftur í vatnið,*' he cried. The warriors all laughed.

'Something about little fish, I think,' translated Mitzi.

Aifa and her father came forward. Aifa's father bowed to the chief. With lowered head, he spoke at length to the older man, pointing to each of the children in turn.

The chief listened carefully. He turned to Aifa, who was bowing so low that she almost had her face in the grass.

'I don't think her father is so important as she told us,' said Jacky to his brother.

The chief asked Aifa a question. She ran over to Oscar and took him away from the man holding him. She held his arm in a fierce grip.

'Hann er minn!' she said.

'She says Oscar is hers,' commented Mitzi. 'It's like he's her pet!'

The chief thought about it, then shrugged and nodded. Aifa offered a huge smile, bowed, and took Oscar away from the others.

'Bindið þá. Komdu með þá,' he commanded. Several of the warriors sprang to obey, and soon the children were sitting in a circle, with their hands tied behind them, watched by two strong and fierce looking Vikings. All except Oscar, who was sitting with Aifa in the group of men that included her father. She was feeding him slices of meat. One of the men handed her a drinking horn, which she offered to Oscar. He took it and drank thirstily from it. Then he choked. The men laughed, one of them spoke:

'Hann er ekki hrifinn af víni!' He grinned.

'Oscar seems to be doing all right,' said Ruby bitterly. 'What are we going to do, Ingrid?'

'Stay calm, everybody. Just try to get the ropes loose, but don't let them see.'

One of the Viking men came over and put down a large wooden platter with lumps of meat and bread on it. He also placed a pitcher down in front of them. Then he squatted down behind Mitzi and cut her bonds.

'Þú gefur þeim að borða,' he said, and he mimed feeding the children.

Mitzi caught on and she picked up lumps of meat and bread from the wooden platter and fed them to her brother and sisters. They had to eat from her hand.

'Yuck,' said Ruby. 'It's really salty, what is it?'

'It's salted meat, I expect,' said Ingrid. 'Eat it. I bet the bread is dry too, but you must eat it. Watch out for green bits. Don't eat those! We need to keep our strength up. We must keep our eyes open for any chance to get away. We have to go back to those rocks. It's our only chance to get back to our own time!'

– CHAPTER SEVEN –

TRAPPED IN THE MIDDLE OF A BATTLE

After Mitzi had fed them all, the warrior took away the little food and water that was left. Jacky noticed something about the man.

'He's only got one hand!' he said. 'Did you see? I wonder if it was chopped off in a fight!'

Ruby pulled a face. 'I wish you hadn't told me that, Jacky. Now I feel sick!'

The warrior turned to him and said, '*Sofa núna!*' He was carrying the platter in his good hand, with the pitcher under his arm, so he mimed the action with his other arm. Another warrior came up and tied Mitzi up again.

'Sleep!' said Mitzi, interpreting the gesture. 'I suppose sofa means sleep. It's a good name for it. Daddy often sleeps on the sofa when we watch a film!'

'Lie down, everybody, make yourself as comfy as you can, and sleep. Tomorrow, we're going to escape!' ordered Ingrid.

Unfortunately, her plans were thrown into chaos. First of all, it was difficult to get to sleep. They were uncomfortable, the ground was hard and their hands were tied behind their backs. In the end, they managed to doze for a bit, but were awoken by loud shouting.

'Saxar!'

Horns were blown, the warriors clattered together their spears, swords, and shields.

The children immediately jumped to their feet. The sun was just below the horizon and light was growing fast.

'The local people must be fighting back,' said Ingrid, yawning. Their one-handed waiter came to them.

'Saxar fyrd,' he said with a hiss.

The Vikings responded to the threat like a well-oiled machine. The warriors formed a wedge formation, with the chief at the centre. One of his men walked over to the chief and spoke to him. He pointed to the children. Minutes later, each child was lifted up by a strong Viking warrior and carried to the centre of the wedge. The Vikings all gazed up to the top of the ridge. Dilly raised her eyes and gawked with them. Everything went completely quiet for a moment, then the ridge looked like it had sprouted a forest, where the tops of spears came into view. There was a collective gasp as row on row of men appeared carrying spears, shields and pitchforks, axes, and scythes. The local lord had arrived with his *fyrd,* a mix of professional soldiers armed with spears and shields and local people, armed with whatever they could get.

'There's hundreds of them!' cried Jacky.

'And they're so close!' said Dilly. The Saxons were barely forty meters away. Still, nobody moved.

'We're dead!' wailed Ruby.

Around three hundred men lined the ridge and stood looking down at the boatload of about fifty Vikings and seven children.

The chief spoke to his men. They hefted their spears. The Saxons began to come down the ridge – the soldiers with their spears and shields at the front, the peasants with their crude weapons behind. They formed a long crescent, with the two wings moving faster than the centre, intending to encircle and trap the Vikings between the *fyrd* and the river. The Viking chief cried out in a great booming voice. Half of the Viking chevron launched their spears over the heads of the first rank of soldiers, into the people behind, most of whom had no shields. This provoked a great shout from the Saxons, and they charged, but the spears had found their mark, and there were many injuries among the fyrd.

A few of the Vikings broke out of the chevron, and back towards the ship. They released the anchor and pushed the longboat into the water. It floated free, dragging a rowing boat behind it. The Vikings, in strict formation, marched rapidly backwards towards the boat, all the time facing the enemy. Those who had thrown their spears scrambled aboard. Those who still had spears left to throw, now hurled them at the Saxon front line. The spears stuck in the Saxon shields, making them heavy and unwieldy. The Saxon soldiers were forced to throw them down.

The retreating wedge of the thirty Vikings who remained on land was faced, barely ten metres away, by more than two hundred angry Saxons. The chief shouted again. The men on the boat stood up with bows. They unleashed them into the front line of the Saxon soldiers, many of whom now had no shields to protect them. Their attack faltered. This gave the remaining Vikings a chance to scramble aboard the ship and cast off from the shore.

Half the men rowed out into the middle of the broad river, while the other half fired arrows into the Saxon ranks. Spears and arrows came back the other way, and it was a dangerous few minutes for everyone on the boat. The children kept their heads down as war cries and weapons flew through the air.

The bowmen put down their weapons and joined the others at the oars, rowing with the current of the river. The longship began to move more and more swiftly. Soon it was going faster than a man could walk, then faster than a man could run.

After some time, the chief called out again, and they stopped rowing, allowing the boat to drift in the current. The men bent over their great long oars, exhausted.

The ship was brought to a stop in the middle of the river and men threw down the stone anchors. The exhausted men looked up from their oars and cheered. They had left the Saxons far behind.

Soon, as they recovered from their exertions, the level of chatter began to rise. Wine was passed around. Even the children were offered some. Ingrid told everyone to refuse.

'No,' she said. 'No wine. We need clear heads.

Besides, you're all too young.'

'Oscar had some!' complained Jacky.

'Yes, and look at him now!' exclaimed Dilly. Oscar was sitting in the belly of the boat with Aifa. He had his head in his hands and he was groaning. She was laughing at him and consoling him in equal measure. Some of the warriors were looking at him and jeering:

'Aifa, Aifa, kastaðu litla fiskinum þínum til baka!' said Aifa's father with a smile.

'He just told Aifa to throw her little fish back,' said Mitzi, who had done a lot of listening to the Vikings' speech.

Jacky was rocking backwards and forwards with more and more urgency. He pulled at the leg of a passing warrior.

The man looked at him. Jacky did a mime. The warrior laughed heartily and called to the others.

'He vill pissa!'

There was no need for Mitzi to translate that! The man lifted Jacky up in one hand and carried him to the prow of the boat. He indicated that Jacky should do what he needed to do over the side of the boat, and cut his ropes, freeing his hands. Blushing like the red sun of morning, Jacky did as he was told. He came back to his sisters where he was tied up again. 'We're out of the frying pan and into the fire,' said Ruby. 'We escaped a battle, but now we're on a boat, ready to be taken who knows where, and we'll probably be forced to live like Vikings!'

– CHAPTER EIGHT –

UP THE CREEK WITHOUT A PADDLE

The chief sent out many of his men on lookout duty. Some of them roamed for quite a distance to make sure there were no Saxons nearby.

Mitzi noticed Oscar pull Aifa away to a quiet area of the boat. Most of the men were taking the opportunity to nap in the warmth of this late August afternoon. Some were sitting repairing the sail, with one or two sharpening their weapons. No one (except Mitzi) noticed as Oscar urgently mimed to Aifa.

Aifa looked surprised and shook her head. Oscar repeated it and held her hands, clearly pleading with her. Mitzi then saw something shocking. Aifa was crying! There were tears rolling down her face as she sat with Oscar, holding his hand. Then, with a sudden movement, she pulled him to her and kissed him on the cheek. She stroked his face. She turned away, put her hand into her bag, and passed him something behind her back. Then she hung her head and sobbed quietly. Oscar put his arm around her, but she sat wrapped in misery.

Time wore on.

Soon the sentries were changed over, the children were given food, and the sun sank in the sky. By eight o'clock it was gone. The shadows were lengthening. The sentries changed over once more. The men settled down to sleep, except for the sentries onshore.

Oscar went towards the front of the boat as if he needed a wee. He didn't look at the others as he passed, but as he walked by there was a quiet clatter. Something had landed on the rope bundle next to Ingrid. She looked down. It was her mother's knife. She leaned over and grabbed it and began to cut through the ropes binding her wrists. Aifa's honing techniques had left the knife as sharp as a razor. She felt strand after strand of the rope break.

At long last, the final thread broke, and her hands were free. She didn't dare move for a moment. She stayed still to get her breath back, massaging the life back into her hands and wrists. As she lay there, the last glow of daylight faded, and under a cloudy sky, it became quite dark. The guards, who were supposed to be keeping an eye on them, didn't appear to consider that they would try to escape. They were not paying attention to the children at all, just playing dice – again!

Ingrid wondered if they were the same two who should have been guarding the boat when Aifa slipped away! She shuffled inch by inch towards Ruby and nudged her.

'Ruby,' she whispered.

'What?' whispered Ruby in an irritated tone. Ingrid had woken her up.

'I have a knife! Just sit still and I'll cut your ropes.'

One by one the Chans had their bonds cut. Aifa walked past the Chans with not a word or a look, and quickly grabbed Ingrid's arm and pulled it. Ingrid's untied arm came free. A tear rolled down her face and she said in a cracked voice, *'Kveðja, Inge'.*

'I think that means goodbye,' said the ever-helpful Mitzi.

'Yes, Mitz,' Ingrid said. 'I think it does.' She pulled Aifa to her and hugged her. *'Kveðja, Aifa!'* she said.

Aifa stood up and moved into the darkness. In a moment Oscar arrived.

'Did you say *Kveðja* to her?' said Mitzi. Oscar just nodded, unable to speak, his face a picture of misery.

He squatted down. No one seemed to be taking any notice of them at all.

'Aifa gave them all some strong wine,' Oscar said. 'They'll sleep for hours.'

'Have you learned Icelandic?' asked Mitzi.

'We did most of it using sign language,' replied Oscar. This made the girls smile. Oscar did not smile. Jacky came and sat next to him.

'When it's really quiet,' Oscar told them, 'Aifa will come. We have to get in the little rowing boat, then we can row to the shore and go back to the rocks again.'

Ingrid nodded, but secretly she was thinking, *it must be more than ten miles back to those rocks and we're tired already. I don't know how we're going to manage it.*

They waited in the darkness. The only sounds were the snores and the flow of the river under the hull of the ship.

Aifa arrived as promised. She led them past the slumbering warriors to the stern. Their hearts were in their mouths, but Aifa's wine had done its job. No one stirred. The sentries were focused on the shore, looking for marauding Saxons. They did not see them attempting the tricky climb over the dragon carving at the rear of the boat and down into the swaying little rowing boat.

Aifa cast off the rope, and they were free. The children frantically held the boat off from the ship, so that it didn't scrape and alert the sentries. It made its way eastwards downstream.

'Come on, Ruby, we'll take the first stint at rowing,' said Ingrid.

There was a moment's silence. Then Ruby, in a small voice, said, 'Inge, I can't!'

'Why not?'

'There aren't any oars.'

'What?'

'No oars. I've looked over the whole boat!'

They were in trouble. They were in the middle of an increasingly fast flowing river, with no way of steering, no way of getting to the shore, and every moment taking them further from home.

'What are we going to do?' wailed Ruby.

Ingrid adjusted her invisible captain's hat. 'Look, we just need to get to shore. Then we can start walking back to those rocks.'

'But how will we get to the shore?'

Ingrid turned to Dilly and the twins. 'Time for some wild-water swimming. Dilly, you get in the water at the stern, act as a rudder. Jacky and Oscar, you get in the water at the bow and push us towards the bank.' The three strongest swimmers looked at each other and hesitated.

'The platoon is counting on you,' said Ingrid, in full captain mode. Dilly shrugged. 'Come on, you two. Think yourselves lucky it's not winter!' she said, slipping over the stern of the little boat into the river.

'It's n-not too c-cold,' she said with a splutter. She swung her body around to the right, pulling the boat with her. The boys followed Sergeant Dilly's lead. They slid into the water at the bow, and splashed with their legs, pushing the bow towards the bank. Dilly straightened herself out to make sure the boat was going in the right direction. She pushed and kicked; the twins pushed and kicked; and the boat began to make headway against the current.

'Well done, you three!' praised the captain.

They all splashed ashore, then Ingrid waded out a little way and pushed the boat back into the stream, where it bobbed away into the night.

'We must brush away our footprints. Ruby, Mitzi cut some branches from the bushes. Use this knife.' They covered up their traces as best they could in the semi-darkness. Then they trudged a little way from the riverbank and lay down in a little grove of trees to get some sleep.

It was Mitzi who woke first. Ingrid awoke to find

Mitzi shaking her.

'Shh!' said Mitzi, who indicated that Ingrid should follow her.

They peeped out from beneath the trees. They were surrounded by two hundred Saxons!

'OMG! Frying pan and fire again!' Ingrid said.

'*Andstandan*!' said a loud voice.

Two men had come up behind them. Out of the frying pan indeed!

– CHAPTER NINE –

A DIFFICULT JOURNEY

The children were prodded out into the open at spear point.

'Etneas,' a Saxon told his colleagues. *'Bearnēacen etneas.'* He held up five fingers.

Ingrid noticed his fingers. *Five?* she thought. She looked around worriedly. Mitzi had disappeared.

Good old, Mitzi. She is doing her hiding thing. Ingrid smiled to herself. She lifted her head and waited as the fyrd began to close in around them. Then, without warning, she turned and ran back towards the trees. There was no real chance of escape – the Saxons were all around her in no time – but escape was not her plan. She pretended to fall over, pushing her mother's best kitchen knife into a hole under a tree. She stood and waited as the men came up to her. One of the men spoke to her, but she didn't understand a word. Old English was just as hard as Icelandic! He looked like a teenager, not much older than herself.

The young man was smiling. He was quite gentle as he took her arm and led her back to the others.

'Canne âr̂îdan!' the young man remarked cheerfully,

puffing out his cheeks to show that he meant what a good runner she was. Ingrid was pushed gently into a sitting position next to the other Chans and was tied up again.

'Are we better off or worse off?' muttered Ruby.

'Better. One, they're going back the way we want to go, and two, they didn't get Mitzi! I left her the knife. I hope she was watching and picked it up.'

The young Saxon man came over, leading a horse and cart. The cart was loaded with water skins and salted meat, along with bales of hay for the animals. The smell of the heaps of dried meat made the children cough.

There was a woman walking beside the cart. She smiled encouragingly at them and mimed getting up into it. The teenage Saxon soldier knelt down and comically offered them his knee as a step for them to climb up. After a moment's hesitation, Ingrid went first. The woman held her arms to steady her as she climbed up. The young man smiled at her and winked.

Ingrid smiled back. 'Thank you,' she said.

The man laughed. '*Thin cue,*' he said, mimicking her. The woman gave a long wheezy chortle.

'*Thancun eow,*' he replied in old English, and he gave a mock bow. Ingrid blushed and threw herself down on one of the cart's bales of hay. One by one the others joined her.

'Well, that's a different way of taking a knee!' said Ruby. 'I think he likes you, Ingrid. You've got an admirer.'

'Shut up!' said Ingrid, who was now crimson with embarrassment.

'It stinks,' added Ruby.

'Better than walking,' remarked Dilly.

Soon the cart was trundling along, back the way they had come. The professional soldiers marched, as you would expect, but the ordinary Saxons walked along casually, talking and laughing.

'They're glad to be alive, I expect,' whispered Dilly.

'And not working in the Lord's fields!' Ingrid muttered back.

The boys were fascinated by everything they saw around them. The soldiers, the weapons, the peasants with their long overshirts and trousers – leather thongs tied around the legs in criss-cross fashion. Their eyes were everywhere. Jacky made Oscar jump when he grabbed his arm, pinching him in his excitement.

'On the wagon, in front,' he said with a hiss.

'Ow, that hurt! What is it?'

'I saw eyes, looking at us. There's an animal or something on that cart!'

Ingrid heard them. 'Shut up, you idiots, and stop looking at it!'

'Why?'

'Because it's not an animal, you dopes – it's Mitzi! Don't look!'

The boys immediately wanted to check Ingrid's statement, but under her glare they refrained from looking at the cart.

Throughout the long hot day, under a cloudy and muggy sky, the column trudged along, following the course of the river back towards the northwest, with only an occasional break for a brief rest and something to eat.

By nightfall they had covered maybe ten miles.

'Anyone recognise those hills?' asked Captain Ingrid quietly of the others. 'Lieutenant, Sergeant?'

'I think, maybe,' replied Sergeant Dilly. 'That looks a bit like Garres Hill and, that in the distance, might be Pot Haw. I'm not used to seeing them from this side.'

'I think you're right. Ingrid, that means we're nearly home!'

'We'll wait for our chance tonight. Stay close to me. I've a funny feeling something is going to happen.'

The camp settled down for the night. Fires were lit, and animals were roasted: rabbits and chickens. The Saxons were happy to have the children as prisoners. They thought they were Vikings of course, which meant the possibility of a ransom. They smiled at them and patted them on the head. They fed them roast meat and watered them, and let them go to the loo in the bushes by the river, but they watched them like hawks. They didn't untie them. The young man who had helped them onto the cart was especially attentive. Ingrid actually blushed when he came across and fed her some chicken from his plate.

'Oh gross!' muttered Ruby. 'That's so insanitary!'

Dilly was chuckling to herself. 'Mmm. So tasty,' she said with a giggle.

'Quiet, you two!' said an embarrassed Ingrid. 'It's not funny!'

'Yes, it is,' said Oscar, clearly visible in the firelight, grinning from ear to ear.

'Aa-aa-aa, Aifa!' Jacky pretended to sneeze, but

managed to turn it into Oscar's crush's name! Oscar kicked him.

The camp settled down. The fires were banked down, darkness descended. The children lay down as best they could to rest.

They were awoken by the most tremendous noise: war cries, shouts, and calls to arms.

'Vikingar! Vikingar!' The Vikings had taken them by surprise and ambushed their camp.

In the middle of the chaos, out of the darkness, Mitzi appeared, armed with the kitchen knife. She cut their bonds. They were free but caught in the middle of another vicious battle.

'This way!' shouted Mitzi and commando crawled, as Ingrid had taught them, away from the action.

'Follow her, everyone, stay in line!' ordered Ingrid.

Mitzi picked her way unerringly through the noise and the fighting. When it was clear they were outside the battle zone, they stopped to catch their breath. After a minute, they were off again. 'Come on!' cried Mitzi. They got to their feet and ran, following their youngest sister.

In the dark, and with all the confusion, the others had not seen where she was taking them. They were all exhausted by the time Mitzi called a halt by a rocky outcrop. A figure loomed up out of the darkness.

'Inge? Oskar?' said a familiar voice.

'It's all right everyone, it's Aifa,' said Mitzi. *'Hæ, Aifa. Allt gott?'* It was indeed Aifa, carrying a very grown-up spear, with a small shield.

There was no time to enquire as to how this miracle

had happened!

'You must tell us all about this later,' said Ingrid.

'Hæ, Mitzi. Ertu með hnífin?' asked Aifa, holding out her hand.

'Ja. Já, hér,' replied Mitzi, as her brothers and sisters looked on in astonishment. Mitzi held out the knife and Aifa tucked it into her belt.

'Þakka þér hjálpina,' continued Mitzi.

'Það var ekkert' Aifa held out her arms. *'kveðjum,'* she said.

Everyone hugged Aifa. They all said *'kveðjum',* all except Mitzi who said, 'Bless, Aifa.'

'Bless, Mitzi,' Aifa replied.

The noise of battle started to get closer. *'Farðu. Farðu hratt'* urged Aifa and hefted her spear and her shield. She turned to face the enemy, the very picture of a battle-hardened warrior!

Mitzi started to explain. 'She means…'

'Run?' asked Ruby. Mitzi nodded. And they ran.

– CHAPTER TEN –

MITZI EXPLAINS

With the noise of battle getting louder and louder behind them, Ingrid spotted a safe space.

'Quick, oh quick!' panted Ingrid. She guided them into the crack in the rocks. Like the good captain she was, she was the last one in, and only just in time. As she entered the passage, Viking warriors chased Saxons around the corner towards her.

After a long walk, the children pushed their way to the centre of the rock cluster. The familiar sick and dizzy feeling came over them, and they fell unconscious to the ground. When they awoke, they were lying under a cloudless blue sky, and there was no sound, except the occasional mournful hoot of a short-eared owl, hunting in the late afternoon.

They made their groggy way out to the opposite side of the outcrop. Ingrid dug in her jeans pocket and produced her phone. She turned it on. There was an agonising few seconds while it warmed up. Then it lit up. It showed the date and the time.

'It's working. We're home!' she exclaimed. 'And it's the same day we came here! We've come back to the very same day. I don't understand. We spent three days in the past.'

'That means Mum and Dad won't even have missed us,' said Jacky. 'Yay! We're not in trouble!'

'Jacky, we've been kidnapped by Vikings, taken prisoner for ransom by Saxons, we've been in the middle of two battles, and you're worried about what Mum is going to say because we're late?' said Ruby.

That made everybody giggle. They all fell on the ground laughing with relief. Although there was sadness, too. Especially for Oscar and Ingrid.

'I really liked her!' pouted Oscar. Ingrid nodded.

'I know, Oscar,' she said. 'And if it's any consolation I think she liked you! I liked her too.'

Ingrid phoned her mother. 'Hi, Mummy. Do you want the good news or the bad news?'

'Oh goodness, give me the bad news quickly,' replied Mum.

'Well, your knife is lost forever! The good news is, Aifa is back home where she belongs, although I think she broke Oscar's heart.'

'You've only been gone a few hours. Is everything OK?'

'Yes, Mum, everything's fine, but once again Mitzi was the hero. We'll tell you about it when we get home. We're by the river near Coniston Cold.'

'Hang on. Can you get to the church? I'll pick you up. I'll be with you in twenty minutes.'

'Oh, thank God for the twenty-first century, for cars, and phones... and baths!' cried Dilly as Ingrid hung up the phone.

'And a hairbrush, and all my nice clothes!' said Ruby.

'And cheese and pickle rolls!' said Oscar.

'Well, you're feeling better!' remarked Ingrid.

'What? I'm hungry!' said Oscar.

They trooped wearily to the church in the village of Coniston Cold and plumped themselves on the wall in the sunshine to wait for the family 'bus' to arrive.

'Well, Mitz, I mean, *Ensign* Mitzi. You have to tell us. How did you do it? Exactly what happened?'

'I remembered what you said last year about those diver things,' said Mitzi.

'Diver things?'

'She means diversions. Do you remember, when we were pretending to hide from the Mercury delivery driver. You told Oscar and Jacky to create a diversion, so we could get away.'

'And you remembered that?' Ingrid was amazed.

'Yes. Anyway, I knew we needed a diver… thingy, so when we camped for the night, I went to find the Vikings. I followed the river until I saw their camp. It wasn't far. I hid until I could get Aifa on her own. She went off by herself to do a wee-wee. She was really surprised to see me!'

'I bet she was!' said Dilly with a laugh. 'Not the best time for someone to pop up out of the grass!'

'How did you get her to understand?' Ruby wanted to know.

'I remembered what they all shouted when the English people came. So, I said '*Saxar*! And I pointed where you were. And I said *'Oskar, Inge'* and I showed her your hands were tied, like this.' She demonstrated. 'She said *'við munum ráðast.'* I think that means they would attack because she did some spearing things with her arms! She went back to her daddy, and I saw them talking, and Aifa was pointing where you were. So, I came back. When they *ráðast*-ed, I cut your ropes with mummy's knife.'

'Well done, Ensign Mitzi. There'll be a medal for you, for this!'

'Can it be made of chocolate please?' That made everybody laugh.

'Yes, I'll buy some chocolate and we can all share it.' Ingrid hugged Mitzi.

'What's happened to your lisp, Mitz?' Dilly wanted to know.

'Oh, I got fed up with it!' said her youngest sister. 'It stopped ages ago, but I kept it going, because I thought you all liked it.'

As they were all laughing at this Mum arrived in the car. They all piled in.

'Tell me about it when we get home!' Mum said.

– CHAPTER ELEVEN –

POSTSCRIPT

Ingrid's heart was in her mouth. It was the day before school. She wandered around the house, not feeling like doing very much. The twins were taking an old clock apart in the quiet room, Ruby was reading to Mitzi in the living room, Dilly was experimenting with iron filings. Ingrid tracked down Mum in her little office.

'Hi, sweetheart. Just come and look at this. I was doing some research into Vikings. Guess what I found?' Ingrid shrugged. Mum turned her laptop round for Ingrid to see.

The Internet was open at a page about Viking settlements in Yorkshire.

Tharlesthorpe was the heading.

'Look at this,' said Mum. 'It seems that Tharlesthorpe was a village recorded in the Domesday Book. The village was founded over a hundred years before that by a Viking raider who settled down with his wife. His name was Tharle. It seems that he had married a female Viking warrior of legend. She had been at the forefront of many battles according to the legends, but the legend says she had been 'tamed' by falling in love with Tharle. Together they founded the village. She was an early Christian convert and had a church built in the village. Her name was Aifa Tharleswyf. That can only be one person, can't it!'

Ingrid stared at the page for quite a few minutes. Slowly a big smile spread across her face.

'She was a famous warrior. She founded a village and a church!' she said. That cheered her up no end. She went in search of Dilly to help her with her chemical experiments.

That night, she was reading in bed before going to sleep.

'Ingrid,' came a voice. She looked around her bedroom in some puzzlement. The door was closed, the room was empty, no one under the bed. Her eyes narrowed.

'Ingrid!'

She crept over to the door and threw it open, book in hand, ready to clout whichever of her brothers was messing about, but there was no one there. She looked up and down the corridor. She padded silently down the flight of stairs that led to the second floor and her brothers' room. She opened the door. There was no doubt about it, they were fast asleep.

'Ingrid!' came the voice, a bit more urgently. 'Ingrid, can you hear me?' She shut the twins' door and tiptoed quietly away. 'Yes, I can hear you,' she said. 'Who is this?'

'Don't you recognise my voice, my faithful counsellor?'

'Aramantha? Is that you?'

There was a chuckle.

'Of course it's me. Who else is going to be speaking through your implant!'

'Oh, of course!' Ingrid said with a gasp. She had forgotten all about the implant!

'You go away to learning soon?'

'Tomorrow.'

'I go to be married tomorrow.'

'Oh. Er, congrat, um, well… that is, good luck!' Ingrid went back to her room and sat on her bed.

'Good luck to you, Ingrid. I will contact you again one day and tell you what it is like to be married. And you can tell me about school. I know you will do well. Do not be nervous. You can face anything. I know, I have seen it!'

'Oh, Aramantha, I'm glad you, er, contacted me. I know you will be fine, too. Just make sure to show him who's boss.'

'I will,' said Aramantha in her head, with a hint of a chuckle in her voice. 'Goodbye, Ingrid. One day we will meet on my world!'

'Bye, Aramantha.'

Ingrid settled down to sleep, feeling much braver than she had earlier.

The big day finally arrived. Ingrid was up early. She showered and dressed in her new uniform. Her things were packed in her trunk, which her dad had put in the car the night before. When she came down, she was carrying a large carrier bag. Early as she was, everyone was there waiting for her. There was a burst of applause as she walked into the kitchen. There was a big banner across the room, which said 'Goood luck, Ingrid!!'

Everyone hugged her and gave her last minute presents.

She stood facing them. 'All right, troop, line up!' she barked. Captain Ingrid was in command!

There was some confusion, as they fought to get into line.

'What a shambles!' she rasped out. 'Tennn... wait for it... shun! That's better! Ensign Mitzi, one pace forward, march!' She fished in the carrier bag and brought out a huge chocolate medal covered in gold foil. 'This is for exceptional bravery and initiative in the face of impossible odds! You are promoted to mission specialist: languages.' Everyone clapped as she placed the medal around Mitzi's neck.

'Sergeant Jacky, and Sergeant Oscar, one pace forward! This is for bravery and fortitude in the highest traditions of the service, even going against personal feelings...' She looked at Oscar and smiled. He blushed. '...for the sake of the troop and the mission. Lieutenant Dilly, step forward and receive your medal, for maintaining morale in the most difficult of circumstances. And finally, Lieutenant Ruby, I promote you to captain of the troop. For support and loyalty against all odds, here is your medal.'

Then it was time to go. The school was in Skipton, less than two hours away by car.

Everyone looked despondent, as they all said goodbye and good luck to her

'Don't worry, everybody, I'll be back in a fortnight.' She smiled. Then they were off. The family waved the 'bus' out of sight.

All too soon they were there. They drove through the gates between old grey stone walls.

Why it's just like Malory Towers! thought Ingrid.

The new girls and their families milled around outside the main building, waiting to be invited in. A girl came over to Ingrid.

'My name is Amrik. What's yours?' she said.

'Ingrid.'

'Hi, Ingrid. Are you nervous?'

'A bit.'

'I'm nearly wetting myself!'

'I'm sure it will be all right.'

'I feel better now I've met you.'

Just then the school secretary came out into the reception hall, and said, 'All right, everyone. Say goodbye to mummies and daddies, and I'll take you into the hall.'

Mum and Dad hugged Ingrid. Ingrid was surprised to see tears in her mum's eyes.

'Don't forget your phone, darling.'

When Dad hugged her, he whispered. 'We're not far away if you need us.' And he pressed some money into her hand.

The secretary came back. Her smile looked like it was glued on, her expression didn't change as she spoke, 'All right, year sevens, come on.'

Just as she turned away, her face changed, very briefly, before the smile came back as if it was floating on the surface of the face.

Ingrid gasped in recognition. Then she set her jaw, checked her invisible ray gun, and followed the others into the hall. It looked as if there was going to be work for Colonel Ingrid of Space Patrol!